AAAAAAAAAAAAAAAAAAAAAAAA

CEREMONY OF THE PANTHER

CEREMONY
OF THE
PANTHER

LUKE WALLIN

AN AUTHORS GUILD BACKINPRINT.COM EDITION

The Ceremony of the Panther

All Rights Reserved © 1987, 2001 by Luke Wallin

AN AUTHORS GUILD BACKINPRINT.COM EDITION

Published by iUniverse.com, Inc.

For information address:
iUniverse.com, Inc.
5220 S 16th, Ste. 200
Lincoln, NE 68512
www.iuniverse.com

ISBN: 0-595-19275-0

Printed in the United States of America

∧∧∧∧∧∧∧∧∧∧∧∧∧∧∧∧∧∧∧∧∧∧∧∧

for Dennis and Tom

This novel is a work of fiction set in recent history. Names, characters, places, and incidents are either the products of the author's imagination or are used fictitiously. Any references to historical events; to real people, living or dead; or to real locales are intended only to give the fiction a setting in historical reality.

Research into the Miccosukee heritage reveals a rich history of the roles of the panther and the deer in contexts of medicine, spiritual identity, hunting magic, and political sovereignty. Care has been taken, in fictionalized scenes of ritual, not to reveal any actual words spoken by real Miccosukee healers.

The rendering of the interior lives of the fictional characters does not reflect an implicit authorial claim to intimate cross-cultural knowledge, but rather the long struggle I have shared with the two men to whom this is dedicated, to participate correctly in another spiritual tradition.

-L.W.

Contents

▲▲▲▲▲▲▲▲▲▲▲▲▲▲▲▲▲▲▲▲▲▲▲▲1

The Healing

Moses Raincrow carried the panther over his shoulders. It weighed a hundred and seventy pounds and its tail drooped to the grass, but Moses' walk was steady up the marshy trail from the water. John followed his father, carrying the rifle across his left arm, his eyes fixed on the long limber body of the taupe-colored cat. It was a beautiful clear morning on the Everglades island, and as they passed through tall sawgrass and cattails, beneath a hawk circling very high against a puff of cloud, the panther seemed impossible. Yet here it was, real and springy over Moses' hard muscular shoulders, proof of the bargain that lived between John's father and the Sky Spirits. The way this big male had come to them told of something else, too, beyond doubt. Without John's vision, they never would have found him.

In a few moments they were within sight of camp, and as they approached they saw Anna, John's mother, running to meet them.

"You have him!" she cried.

Moses nodded and smiled.

"That's wonderful!" she said, out of breath when she reached them. "But listen, Grandmother Mary's unconscious. She's been this way for an hour already."

"How's her breathing?" Moses asked, already starting to run.

"It's all right. She looks peaceful, but I just can't wake her up."

Anna hurried back with Moses and John, watching the panther's big head flop up and down as Moses ran.

"She was talking about the panther," Anna said as they approached the old woman. Moses dropped to his knees beside Grandmother Mary, and let the cat slide heavily down his back to the ground. "She was saying again how much she needs the ceremony."

They looked at her ancient, wrinkled face. It was wide and copper-colored, a classic Miccosukee face. Even though part of her soul was somewhere else, John felt her strong presence here now.

"I'm not going to wait," Moses said.

"You mean you won't skin him first?"

"No! No time, son. Get my medicine box."

John hurried to the old trunk where Moses kept his things and grabbed the little cypress box. Moses stepped to the smoldering star fire. The five logs were barely touching. He pulled them closer together, to build the flame. "Go get fresh water," he said, handing John the cast-iron pot.

By the time he'd returned from the canal, Moses had already dragged the panther close along his grandmother's side. John hung the black pot from its tripod over the fire, and in a few minutes it was bubbling loudly. Moses took the *toli*, the bay leaves that didn't grow this far south, from his box and dropped them in. He added *ichakcobi*, sunbonnet, and bits of the inner bark of *icintohani*, deer's peach, and of *icisalali*, deer's bean.

When it was all boiling together Moses carefully lifted it from the fire and set it down on the ground beside Grandmother Mary. Gently, he smoothed back her hair and turned her head so that she wasn't facing west, the burial direction. Then, facing east, he rinsed his mouth with a cup of clean water.

He inserted his hollow cane tube beneath the surface of the hot brew and blew into the liquid. In this way, the living medicine in his body passed through his breath and down inside the steaming pot.

Quietly, so not even his wife and son could hear, Moses recited the secret spell of the living deer, and he blew again into the cane.

In a moment he spoke the spell of the dead deer, and again he blew his cleansed and power-carrying breath into the mixture.

Now he held the pot near the old woman and waved it beneath her right arm. He rubbed the herbal steam into the folds of her soft skin, then onto her forehead and cheeks. When he had prepared both arms and raised her long skirt to massage the calves of her legs, he put down the pot and lifted the panther's right foreleg.

"To the living deer," he whispered, "my words have been said."

He placed his broad hand over the panther's huge front paw and pulled the skin sheaths back. Then he placed the sharp curved claws high on Mary's arm.

"To the dead deer," Moses intoned, "my words have been said."

He raked the claws sharply down her arm, all the way to her wrist. Blood rose instantly and filled the deep scratches.

He pulled on the panther's hind legs until its head was even with Mary's waist. Then he lifted her skirt to her knees and dragged the exposed claws along the veiny backs of her calves. He carved all the way to her ankles.

"To all of them," he spoke as softly as the breeze in the switchcane, "my words have been said."

He lifted the cat and placed him along Mary's other side, and repeated his ministrations. "To all of them," he said finally, "I have made it clear. I have said that the panther is coming! He's coming! And when he comes, you are not safe! Leave this woman's body! Leave now! Leave now, or be eaten when he comes!"

Moses was sweating and shaking a little as he laid the panther down for the last time. Grandmother Mary lay motionless, bleeding from the many scratches, and her eyes were growing tight

with wrinkles, as if pain were reaching her in some
far-off place. Her mouth was beginning to twist.

Moses rose and looked at his wife and son. "I've
done all I can," he said. "At least I know that."

They nodded.

"Now, Anna, if you'll watch over her, John will
help me with the cat."

ᛉᛉᛉ They carried the panther to the clearing in
the palmetto and sawgrass, where a solitary spreading live oak stood. Then they tied his back paws,
threw the ropes over a thick black limb, and hoisted
him up into the air. In a moment he was tied off,
swinging a little but hanging securely, and Moses
took out his curved skinning knife and whetstone
and began to sharpen it. John sat down with the
rifle and opened the breech. He held it up to the
blue sky and looked down the barrel. The breeze
came over them, and in the distance crows called
out. It felt like the most private place in all the great
swamp. John wondered if he would ever be a medicine man like his father. Would he be here doing
this alone, or maybe even with a son of his own,
someday?

Then three men with guns rose from the grassy
marsh and stood staring, wordless—daring Moses
and John to move. Slowly, John realized the tall,
red-haired white man in the center was Crane—
Officer Ron Crane from the Endangered Species
Task Force. He kept his revolver trained over their
heads, as if he didn't want to take a chance on really

shooting them. But his men were another story. *Eldon and Pete*, John remembered bitterly. It made sense that they held long-barreled, pump-action shotguns, each one aimed carefully at Moses' head.

In a tired, angry voice, Officer Crane said, "Well, witch doctor, I see we got here just a little bit too late."

John turned furiously from one to the other of them.

"You be still," Officer Crane said. Then, speaking to his men but without taking his eyes from Moses, he said, "Snap the handcuffs on him first."

They made Moses stand while they locked the steel-gray links around his wrists. He said nothing. As John watched, his father seemed to disappear into his thick, muscular body.

The big man, Eldon, leaned up to his face. "Know what you're gonna get?" he asked.

"To start with," Pete said in his high voice, his shotgun still leveled at Moses, "there's a twenty-thousand-dollar federal fine for killing a panther. Did you know that?"

"There sure is," Eldon added. "There sure is."

"And," Pete continued, "there's a state fine and a jail term. You hear that, mister? You're bound for the jailhouse this time."

Moses straighted up and turned away from them. Furious, John wondered what he could mean by "this time." Moses had never been arrested before.

"You'll get a few years for sure," Eldon said.

"At least," added Pete.

"Shut up," Crane said to his men.

He put his revolver away, and they slowly lowered their shotguns.

"The shame of it is," Crane said, looking at the body of the cat hanging heavily from the tree, "nothing can bring him back now."

"Look who's talking!" John blurted out, remembering the sight of another dead panther. Crane himself had been standing next to it. John's face flushed, and he was amazed at himself.

Crane turned to him and pointed a long finger. "You, boy—how old are you again?"

"Sixteen."

"Yeah, that's right. Get out of here."

"Arrest me, too!" John said.

"Git! Go fetch the air boat," Crane said to his men.

They held a moment longer, glaring at Moses, reluctant about taking their shotguns entirely away from him. John sensed that they hardly ever got to arrest anybody.

Once they had disappeared into the brush, Crane strode up to Moses and gave him a direct stare.

"It was wrong, you know," the white man said quietly.

Moses turned from his eyes and sighed.

"You don't understand anything!" John said.

Crane spun and stabbed a finger at him. "I told *you* to *git!*"

John started along the trail toward his great-grandmother's camp, but when he reached the edge of the clearing he stopped and looked back. He knew it was the last time he would see the panther. And his eyes were on his father's special rifle, which lay in the grass beneath the cat. They would take the rifle, too.

He turned and ran.

ΛΛΛ Grandmother Mary was sitting up beside Anna, before the star fire.

"Look!" his mother called when she saw John coming. "Look who's awake now!"

Grandmother Mary turned slowly to face John, and she smiled. "Come here, boy," she said softly. "I want you to see what the spirits have done today."

"They took him!" John cried.

"What?"

"Papa! They arrested him! They're going to put him in jail!"

"*Who* did?" Anna asked.

"Crane! That man from the Task Force. And two others. They put him in handcuffs. Just like he was a criminal."

Grandmother Mary began to rock back and forth very slowly.

"You were in the clearing?" Anna said, gathering up her shawl.

"Yes. They're already taking him to their air boat."

"I didn't hear it."

"They must have poled in for a long way. But it's somewhere close."

"Stay with your great-grandmother. I've got to go with him."

"No!" John said. "I mean, can't I be with him, too?"

Grandmother Mary began to speak in a droning voice as she rocked. "The white man kills what he wants, and he takes what he wants. All these years now, he said we had the rights to our land out here. Didn't he say that?"

John looked at her and nodded.

"I need you to be here," Anna said. "I'll make them take me in with him, and that way I can try to get some help. Do you understand me?"

"I understand you," John said, "but—"

"No!" she said. "Just do it, please. I *need* you here!"

"All right," John said. "Go on then. Just go on."

"I'm sorry, son." She hurried out of camp.

Grandmother Mary kept speaking, her eyes fixed somewhere out in the palm woods. "The white man said it was up to us, the Miccosukee, to decide when to hunt, when not to hunt."

"That's right, Grandmother."

"But I never believed them. Did I? *Did I, John?*"

"No. You never did."

"So here they are, putting handcuffs on Moses!"

"It makes me so mad I want to kill them," John said.

"*Yes!*" she said. "Of course it does. But we haven't killed one in a long, long time."

John smoothed her hair. "It just makes me so mad."

She put her bleeding arms around him and hugged his waist tightly, holding on.

They heard the loud air boat crank up beyond the clearing.

"At least he healed me," she said. "At least I have that."

John met her eyes and said, "I wish you could have seen the panther, Grandmother."

"This is what's important," she said, holding up her right arm. The skin of matted wrinkles and scratches sagged from her upper arm, but she smiled and hugged him again, and John felt her strength.

"I guess so," he said. "It sure seems to be working."

"Oh, yes. Oh, yes."

She rocked back and forth a little. John looked up at the open sky and listened to the wind in the reeds. He heard Crane's air boat crank and rev a few times as it got going. Its sputtering became a high-pitched whine as it shot away from the island.

The Human Zoo

The beginning of it—of John's time in the swamp, of the hunt for the panther—was a warm night in the early fall.

They had finished supper, and he had taken down the sign that said the pit was still open. But one last Cadillac pulled in, heavy and weighted down with fat white people. They had trouble getting out, and they were laughing and smelled of liquor.

"Wait a minute!" the gray-haired man in the lavender jump suit and the baseball cap yelled at John. "You not closed yet, are you? You got that alligator wrestlin' here? We want to see that. Now, we sure do!"

The others laughed and agreed, slamming their doors with great effort, then smiling in satisfaction at the long hot car. A blue-haired woman pulled out a camera and began trying to focus it on John.

"It's late," he said. Three hours earlier Max had given him the tab of LSD, and the strongest part of his trip was just coming on. The last thing he needed was these turkeys.

"Wait a minute!" the big man cried, hurrying toward him with the too-fast, bent-forward walk of intoxication. He grabbed John's shoulder and squeezed it. "Look," the man said, "we drove all the way down here from Iowa. Imagine that? My wife, and my brother there, and his wife, we really want to see your Indian village inside." He pointed to the thatched fence that screened off the Raincrow family's home from the highway.

"Cheese!" the woman with the camera said, firing off a flash in John's eyes.

He had been about to curse them good. But his father came up behind him, and in a steady voice he said, "Sure, we're open. But you've got to pay my son five dollars for that picture."

"Five dollars!" the woman cried.

"No problem," her husband said. He pulled a ten from his shirt pocket and handed it to John. "Keep the change."

"You want another picture, then?" John asked coldly.

"Naw. One's enough."

"Then I'll get you change."

"I said to keep it, boy," the big white man barked. "God knows you must need it."

John's father grabbed him roughly and pulled him aside. "Look, boy," he whispered loudly, "what's got into you, so high and mighty? You think I like this? You think we don't *need* to do this?"

John jerked away from him and disappeared behind the fence. He hurried through their living area, past the gator pit, and then into the palm shadows beside the deep, black canal. His heart was going too fast, and his stomach was queasy. He knew it was only partly because of these whites, their tourist eyes searching his home. Mostly it was his parents taking money to exhibit themselves, animals in a human zoo. It was bad enough pretending to do anything—eat supper or read his homework—with them watching. John couldn't concentrate in those times—it was all he could stand just to keep his eyes away from them, to say nothing. . . . His father would be angry about the way he'd acted. . . . *Well, tough*, John thought.

As he hid in the darkness beside the water, the night came gently alive with spooky faces. They were moving against the velvet blackness of the air, silently mocking him with huge open mouths.

He heard the tourists exclaiming as they photographed his mother beside her cookfire inside. *Okay then, take your stupid pictures. . . .*

Max Poor Bear's soft whistle came over the dark water. John slipped down to the edge and smiled as his forbidden friend came into sight, letting his jonboat drift and touch the bank. Max lived half a mile away, and they had no trouble meeting after dark, even within hearing of Moses and Anna.

"What you doin'?" John whispered.

Max grinned and handed him an already opened beer.

He took it and drank deeply.

Then he studied the form of his friend in the boat. Max was twenty years old. He was tall and lean, always cool, detached. He made the struggles of most people seem foolish. John had never known him to work a regular job. He seemed to bring in plenty of cash just from dealing, and selling bull-frogs to restaurants. He passed a serene judgment on all matters, and he made John want to be inside his circle more than anywhere on earth.

John heard the tourists inside as they walked around the pit. "Look at those things!" a woman cried. "They *scare* me!"

"You don't mean you get down in there with them?" a man asked Moses.

They all drew their breaths, and John knew why—Moses was unbuttoning his shirt, then pulling it off. He had a beautiful chest, dark bronze and tight, and his arms were pumped up hard from lifting. He kept in shape for a man forty-four years old. John guessed those white women were willing to pay a lot to see alligators try to eat such a man.

But it would have to be happening just as Max got there, because he always made fun of the show.

John heard the splash of his father landing in the cement moat around the island of sand. And the rough sliding of gator hides on concrete walls as they tried to get away from him. He would have to make his jump quickly now—before the tourists realized how frightened the gators were. And sure enough, John heard the crash and the growling as his father tackled Old George.

"Strong medicine," Max said quietly.

John's face was hot with embarrassment. He killed the beer and held out his hand for another one.

"How's your head?" Max asked.

"Great," John said. "It's good stuff."

"Uh-huh. Told you."

"*Ohhhhh!*" the women cried out, no doubt as Moses rolled over and over with Old George, fourteen feet long.

"John?" It was his mother calling, coming along the path in the darkness.

John took the second beer, sucked down half of it, and quickly gave the can back to Max. He pushed off into the canal and in a few seconds was out of sight.

"What are you doing?" Anna called.

"Nothing."

"Well then, come up here, please. Your father may need you."

"In a minute."

"Not in a minute, John. Come now."

"Just a *minute*, all right?" he said angrily.

He saw her profile at the top of the bank. Her hands were on her hips, her long, black hair braided behind her head. She was getting plump, and she seemed unsettled most of the time lately. Maybe she hated the tourists as much as he did? Maybe his father did, too? He couldn't be sure. It was hard to see how Moses could take this—he was a respected man in council, and out on the reservation they really looked up to him. But here he was.

Anna turned and disappeared without a word.

John heard the white people gasping as Moses and Old George did their splashing rolls.

Then Max was close by, speaking softly. "I'll meet you out here about twelve, okay?"

"Okay," John answered. He was holding a palm tree, wishing he could walk right up its skin and into the night sky.

Slowly, he started to climb the bank trail. But a bullfrog began to sing deeply, and then a dozen others, strung all along the canal, answered in their pulsing voices. John grabbed the rough palm and nodded his head with the music. They were singing directly to him, and as he listened he floated right on out of his body. It was heavy, anyway, and the bullfrog chorus was lighter than air. Their droning was so easy and bassy and rhythmic. John's consciousness hovered over the canal with the overlapping notes, invisible and weightless, and it came to him like a mystical surprise: *these frogs . . . they're high all the time!*

Not in My House

When John passed the gator pit and entered the circle of chickees, he heard water running in the shower by the outside shed. His father was cleaning up. John smelled the hamburger his mother had fried, and the potatoes.

"They're gone now," she said. "Been gone. Come and eat something."

He stood there smelling and smelling the cooked meat, until his father was beside him, clean and soap-scented, his black hair wet. He was shaking John's shoulder gently. "Hey, son, what is it?"

John looked into his eyes and laughed.

"He's on something," his father said to his mother.

The next thing John knew, he was being led to the table, and there was a plate set before him. Hot steam was rising into his face from the hamburger in its soft, seeded bun.

"Can you eat?" his mother asked.

"Sure can," he heard himself say. He was laughing as he lifted the sandwich, spilling drops of catsup on his lap and then smearing it on his face as he took a huge bite.

"My god," his father said. "What are you on this time?"

But John was flying. He was far beyond these little people stuck to the skin of the earth, rooted beside this highway.

And the food! It was wonderful, a world of tastes, a red onion slice beneath the lettuce, a thick wedge of tomato, and the juicy hot beef against the fluffy bread. It made no sense that his parents were raising their voices.

"You should see yourself," his father said.

And there was a steady background noise, not just the high-beating tree frogs and beneath them, in the distance, the magical bullfrogs. There was a coarser sound, a choking and crying. Mama crying.

John looked up, eyes glazed, his grin fixed in place. *Why can't they just relax and enjoy this moment? Why can't they leave me alone with this fantastic hamburger?*

"So," his father said slowly, "you think you'll let me wrestle the alligators, and you'll take the drugs, eh?"

John dropped his sandwich and heard it fall beside the plate.

"You bring me down, man," he said.

Moses slammed his fist on the table, and pieces of the hamburger jumped in different directions.

"Look at this! Look at this!" his mother was

saying. But John couldn't take his gaze from his father. Moses' eyes were glowing.

"John? Would you *look?*" she sobbed. She pressed something into his palm and folded his fingers over a thin, worn surface. He dropped his chin to his chest.

After a while he realized he was holding a one-hundred-dollar bill.

"This what they gave you for wrestlin' Old George?" he asked.

Moses nodded slowly. He was drawing up into himself, tighter and tighter.

"Was it worth it?" John asked.

Moses was dead still.

"John," Mama said, "do you realize how much we need this money?"

"A gift from the Sky Gators?" he sneered.

Moses' stool crashed over backward as he rose.

"That what it was?" John asked. The light was hurting his eyes, and the walls were melting lines.

Moses came around the table toward him.

"Here you go," John said. He ripped the bill in half. "More of it."

He stood up and held out the pieces in his two hands.

It had been years since Moses struck him, and John didn't expect it, even while he watched his father draw his fist back. It caught John in the middle of his chest and knocked him backward off his feet. He flopped hard on the packed dirt floor, breath missing, no power to suck the air. His mouth was wide open, trying to move even little puffs inside, but his lungs would not fill. His chest was aching now, and he knew it would cave in, explode to the inside. Suddenly, the air rushed in again, and he was on his side, gasping and choking. Waves of aching crossed his ribs, pressed the base of his skull.

"That's it," Moses said, standing over him. "That's all I'm putting up with in my house."

"What do you mean?" Anna said. "What do you *mean* by that?"

"He's gone. He's gone tonight. Pillhead. *Drunk.* Look at him."

"What are you *talking* about?"

"Pack him a few things, Anna. I'm taking him to the reservation."

"What about school?"

"He's not learning anything there. Get his stuff."

"I don't want him out in that swamp. Moses, he needs us."

"Yeah? Maybe. But not tonight. Not for a long time. Pack his stuff or he goes without it."

"I can tape up the hundred-dollar bill," she said. "It's not ruined."

John knew they were talking about somebody else. They had to be. He rolled and tried to get up.

Then they were out of the room, out back somewhere, shouting at each other. *Can he make me do this?* John thought. *Can he really dump me in that godforsaken swamp?*

In another minute his father was jerking him up, throwing him over his shoulder like a sack of feed.

His mother was weeping as Moses walked past. "You don't have to do this," she was saying. "You don't."

But they were already gone. Moses opened his pickup door and shoved John inside. "Don't move," he said, and he slammed the door.

He took the duffel bag from his wife and tossed it in the back.

"You get his boots?"

"I didn't see them," Anna said tearfully.

"*John!* Where're your boots?"

"Max's," he mumbled.

"That's great," his father said. He hurried to his side and climbed in, cranked the engine.

"*I can tape it up!*" Anna cried as he drove off.

Then they were on the Trail highway, moving.

In a moment Moses touched his brakes and turned in at Max's.

"Can you walk?" he asked.

John nodded.

"Get your boots, then. And you make this fast."

John climbed down and stumbled inside, holding his chest.

Max was not in sight. John ran through the chickees, out into the darkness, and down to the bank above the canal.

"Hey, hey, little buddy!" Max said. He was in a lawn chair, smoking a joint.

"Max! He's taking me to the res, man." John sank down in a lawn chair with a torn mesh bottom. "He knocked the crap out of me."

"Wow," Max said.

"You know where my boots are?" John asked, dazed.

"Boots. Yeah, I know. Let me get them and get you out of here. I don't want Moses coming in, you know?" Max disappeared inside. When he returned he handed John the boots with their laces tied together, and before John's eyes he stuffed a small plastic bag down into one toe.

"Blotter Acid, man. From the West Coast. Pretty good liftoff, huh, Johnny?"

"Yeah," John said, far away. "You giving me some more?"

"Uh-huh. In a little bag of grass. Don't forget where it is."

"Okay. Thanks a lot."

"You got any money?"

"I'll get it, Max. You don't have to worry about that."

"I don't, huh? Well, we'll see. That's all you get, so make it last."

"Thanks, man. I owe you."

"You got that right."

"He'll take me out to Mary's island," John said. "I can't get off there unless you help me."

Max nodded, distant and calm.

"When you coming? This stuff won't last long, you know."

"I'll be out, but what are you planning to pay up with?"

"I'll get it, man! I swear I will!" It made John's head hurt to yell.

"Yeah, yeah, okay."

"Don't let me down," John said. "Don't leave me out there."

The horn blew twice.

Max laughed.

John turned to run and Max called after him, "Hey! You got to pay me the next time I see you—better starting thinking about that!"

"Yeah, yeah," John said, shaking. "Just don't forget me out there."

On Mary's Island

Moses didn't try to talk, and John let himself drift back into his acid trip. They drove for hours, and one part of John's mind stayed fixed on his father hitting him, reliving it again and again. Another focus, centered through his eyes, seemed to live in the headlights' glare, in the twin moving spots where the world melted and danced.

Finally, they turned onto the empty res road. As they wound through the lower reservation, John felt the remoteness and darkness of the Everglades closing behind them. That image grew and grew in his mind, as circles within circles of thick palms and pines interlocked and tightened. They were going into the heart of the swamp, into alligator and panther country. And the drugs in his boot were his only way out, his only release until his friend came. *Which had better be soon*, he thought and almost said aloud.

A doe quickly crossed in the lights before them, and Moses braked and skidded, then pulled his truck straight again. That deer was a new vision for John to dwell on, to see blooming before him over and over. In what seemed just a moment, the next hour somehow flashed by. Then they were standing under the brilliant stars, and Moses was helping John up into the passenger seat on the air boat. He smiled, still watching the running doe in his secret mind. With enough acid, the swamp might be quite a ride....

They flew in the incredibly loud machine over the surface of the glades canal. John heard demons of motor and wind screaming in his ears, blasting his hair back, erasing the past. They held him to this instant, to the amplified roaring of the rebuilt Ford engine, and to the ripples of his cheeks in the wind. It seemed that the rush would never end.

But at last Moses cut the engine, and they rocked back and forth on swells of prop wash, drifting into the hidden creek that ran from Grandmother Mary's island. They bobbed up and down in the foamy waves, and John's head was filled with afternoise from the air boat. Roughly, Moses pulled him down and planted his feet in the soft muck of the marsh.

They walked together in silence up to Grandmother Mary's camp, and John barely spoke to her before climbing onto the woven mat of her extra sleeping platform. Moses' voice blended with hers as John drifted away, and he slipped easily into a dream.

The next thing John remembered, he was awake and it was dawn. His mouth was very dry, and he had the sense of important traveling, of visiting another world, but he couldn't remember what it was like. He felt down inside his boots, scraping his fingernails on the rough leather, but the bag was gone.

▲▲▲ Grandmother Mary was watching him, smiling. She was eighty-nine, but she moved around her cooking fire with the quick grace John remembered. Mary was still the only person who knew where some of the secret plants grew in the swamp. John studied her now, wondering how much Moses had blabbed about him.

"Fish soup," she said. "When you're ready."

"It smells good," he said, swinging his legs over the side of the sleeping platform.

John dropped heavily to the ground and stretched, then gave Grandmother Mary Osceola a hug. She had, as always, her good smell of smoke and crushed nuts, and her bronze skin was a fine, tender matting of wrinkles. He was suddenly glad to see her again.

"How've you been doing, Grandmother?"

She touched her legs and squinted tightly. "Deer sickness, John. Down in my joints, in my bones. Rabbit sickness, too, I think. Moses could get rid of it, if he had time! If he *would!*"

"I guess," John said.

"You guess? Is that what young men say today? Don't you *know?*"

John shrugged his thick shoulders and reached

for the dipper in the pot of soup, suspended from the blackened metal tripod over the coals.

"There's only one way to get rid of the deer sickness, John. He's got to scratch me with panther claws! You know that, don't you?"

"Sure," John said, without meeting her eyes.

"He knows the ceremony, because I taught it to him. And he knows the songs. I taught those, too! But the man can't help me without claws, can he, John?"

As angry as John felt toward his father, he couldn't accept Grandmother Mary's belief. This was no Sky Deer plaguing her. She probably had arthritis, and if she really wanted a cure, she'd come out and see a white doctor. But Mary had not left her tiny island in the glades for at least three generations. Younger people barely knew of her, even though she had once been a great medicine woman of the tribe. Moses was preparing himself to follow her in this path, working through his seven-year apprenticeship, trying to learn her spells and remedies before she crossed over.

"Has he mentioned the panther to you?" she asked.

"No, Grandmother."

John blew across the surface of the hot soup.

"Not at all? Not even one time?"

This was Moses' great failure in her eyes, that he had killed no panther. He needed claws and tail and skin and head for his healing rituals.

"He did say something about a place in Montana."

"Oh? What place is that?"

"They sell the skins of mountain lions. I guess he was thinking he might order one. I know he wrote them a letter."

"It won't do any good!" Mary said. "That's not the way a medicine keeper works."

The old Miccosukee world was a dangerous place, full of spirits and enemies and magical warfare. John felt how present it was to Mary. He didn't want to offend her, but he didn't want to discuss it, either. He was embarrassed by his father's involvement with the old religion and by his efforts to teach it to the children of the tribe. Right this minute John was just grateful that Max couldn't see him, listening to Grandmother Mary and pretending to believe she made sense.

"I heard that air boat last night," she said, "and I wished Moses was here to shoot somebody for me."

She waited for John to smile.

"But of course, he'd of had to shoot himself, wouldn't he? And you, too!"

She turned away and sniffed.

"I guess he was in a hurry, Grandmother."

"I guess he was! He's too busy for me, and he's too busy to hunt the panther. I hope he's doing something for somebody!"

"Aw, Grandmother. Leave him alone, will you? He's doing the best he can."

"Is that so? He says he can't do anything with *you* anymore."

John frowned and drank from his bowl of soup.

"Is it true? Are you big enough to make trouble for Moses and Anna now? He said you might drop out of the white man's school."

"Yeah."

"You don't need it anyway. What did you learn in that school?"

"I don't know, Grandmother," he said, annoyed. "Different things."

"You don't need it."

"We had some pretty good times, sometimes. Especially the wrestling. I liked that part the best."

"Were you good at it?"

"*Real* good." He grinned.

"You beat the white boys?"

"Oh, yeah!" John put his bowl down and assumed a wrestling crouch, with his head low and forward, his muscled arms held out wide. "I'd go like this, Grandmother," he said, and he tossed his head back quickly, so that his thick black hair flew up and then flopped forward again. "That psychs 'em out. When they see that hair, they know I'm gonna do something to them. Something bad."

She smiled and nodded her head. "Psychs them out?"

"Makes them scared," John said. "Makes them want to go back home."

"I like this," she said quietly. "This sounds very good to me."

"Yeah, well, that wasn't the whole thing," John said. "That was just wrestling. Anyway, it didn't matter how many white boys I beat, Grandmother, because after high school is over, you know what happens?"

"What?"

"They go to college. For them, wrestling's just something to do for a while. Most of the white boys go right on to college. They might wrestle there, or they might not. But our boys, they just go out to one of the 'villages' by the highway, and sit in the sun all day. They drink whiskey and wrestle alligators for the tourists."

She was silent.

"And get a gut on them."

She thought about this for a moment. "You know," she said, "I've never seen that world."

He nodded.

"I never did want to."

"No, Grandmother."

She came to him and touched his cheek, and her hand was soft and very warm. "You stay out here with me," she said. "Your papa was right."

AAAAAAAAAAAAAAAAAAAAAAAAAA**5**

Storm in the Glades

The first few days were hard. His body ached for the sugar in the alcohol, and as he wandered in the lush jungle he was tormented by images of cold beer and by longing for the space where beer and grass took him. It would have been so easy to lift out of the hot, solid world, which fit him like a prison, like a school. He stayed away from Mary as much as he could; her calmness wasn't right, it wasn't fair. She only *thought* she was calm, because she knew nothing else. *What a misery!* John cried to himself. It was the stupidest thing, to live like this forever, caught within the hours of slow detail....
He watched a turtle sneaking across an alligator's channel, and suddenly the gator rose from beneath the surface and grabbed it up between sharp rows of teeth. John waited and the gator waited, and the hot sun hung in the sky. The air was humid and still, and not even a bird cried out to break the silence. Then the alligator tossed the turtle free, and it scuddled away with long scars down its shell to

mark the day. *That's what happens out here,* John thought. *But nothing changes.*

Grandmother Mary told him to rebuild the sweat lodge on the island, and that was fine because it was away from her camp. As he worked at it, bending green saplings and lashing them together with tough strangler fig vines, he tried to rise to this challenge his father had forced on him. *I'm no junkie, after all,* he thought. *They're not going to look at me like some sick fool. Let the sun shine hot, let it cook me, I don't care.* The dome of poles took shape slowly, with more pieces than he really needed, more knotted ties.

At dusk his boredom was at its worst, rising from the swamp water like a living thing to mock him. The hot fall day he could endure, but when the long evening began, promising to be as seamless and slow as all others, he wanted to give up. If only he could have broken its grip with a few beers beneath the sunset sky, or smoked a little reefer and brought on the night with a buzz. Sundown was the one time he really missed Max and the wildness of the highway scene.

Max was a scuzz for not showing, for not getting him out. He was doing exactly what he liked, every night. *One day he'll want something from me,* John thought. *He'll be sorry then....* But John wouldn't let himself sink too low in front of his great-grandmother. He did sit-ups or slipped away alone to swim up and down, up and down, in the warm canal. He splashed hard to keep the snakes away, and he never stayed in long enough for the gators to come investigate. If he kept busy in her eyes, she wouldn't wonder about his thoughts. She'd never be too sure she really knew him. Maybe she'd even think Moses was wrong to exile such a boy.

When he did join her around the cookfire at night, Grandmother Mary wasted no time in bringing up tribal traditions and her wish that he follow Moses in medicine work.

"There's one thing he needs almost as much as those panther claws," she said one night.

"Oh?"

"That's right. His medicine bundle is wrapped in a deerskin, and it won't last another season. You saw it at the Green Corn Dance, didn't you?"

"Yes."

"Well, then you know."

John waited, feeling something coming.

"He's got to have a new skin, and there's an old buck who's wearing it. You know what I'm saying, now?"

"I know one big old buck...he was really something."

"That's it! The one you and Moses saw a year ago."

"You remember that, Grandmother?"

"Of course I do. I knew then... *that's* the deer for the next medicine bundle. And I thought to myself, John should be the one to take him."

"He was some buck. We counted ten points back then. But the hunters might've gotten him by now."

"No! I can feel it. He's waiting for you. And your father will be so proud when you get him."

John smiled slightly. He had never killed a deer. Max made it sound easy, and he shot them all the time. Usually he was drinking, and a lot of them he killed at long range with his huge rifle. It was different from the way Moses hunted.

"What am I going to use, Grandmother?"

"Don't worry about that! I've got Charlie's rifle, for when the time comes."

John's eyes widened. He had no idea. His great-grandfather's old deer rifle? Still out here in working shape? Living in the swamp began to seem more interesting.

"You know how to prepare yourself?" she asked.

He glanced at her and then into the coals. More mumbo-jumbo. Hunting wasn't simple for her. It was part of a contract between the hunter and Sky Deer.

"Sure."

"Don't say it like that!" she said. "If you don't take the sweat and purify yourself, if you don't pray before the morning you go out...there won't be any Give Away!"

"Okay, Grandmother. All right."

She rocked back a little and squinted at him, thinking. He knew she distrusted him right now, and he doubted she'd really hand over that rifle.

"But this buck," she said, "he's old, like me. He's special. And when you kill him, there's one thing you mustn't do. And this is the most important thing of all."

"What's that?"

"You must not enjoy it! Do you realize that?"

He stood up and looked down on her, his judge.

"You bet, Grandmother," he said, and he headed out into the darkness alone.

ΛΛΛ The weeks passed, and John traveled the canals in Mary's dugout canoe, which old Charlie had carved before he died. John discovered secrets—ibis nests, a bobcat's den, the sharp, sudden coolness of the air before a storm. He found an eerie room created by royal palms a hundred feet high and flooded waist-deep by clean, coffee-colored water. Inside, in the quiet, filtered light, thousands and thousands of white ghost orchids floated among the trees. One afternoon he visited this strange, holy place and saw a black bear standing in the gloom.

Later, still a long way from Mary's island, he gathered pine knots for her fire. The canoe was piled high with them, and he was about to start back when the weather changed. First there was an ozone smell, then the ominous green color spreading over the whole sky. He looked across a great field of bright grass, vast and flat and still, to the tall pines beyond. High above, a black cloud bank was building, showing its soundless rivers of lightning. A few seconds later the thunder would rumble toward him across the air. And as he watched, the mass of storm clouds slowly rose into the deepening green sky.

He didn't want to be caught out here when the lightning came, so he beached the dugout and walked into a dense grove of custard apple trees that grew near the water's edge. He made his way into the center of the trees, where the air was dry and sweet smelling, and he lay down on the cushion of grass and leaves. Soon the crisper breeze stirred over him, and a peal of thunder came a little louder, bouncing through the clouds.

He thought for a long time about the old religion, how it almost made sense out here. But not on the Trail. *No religion made any sense there. Who can really tell what's true anyway? Not me,* he thought, *not me.*

He rolled over and closed his eyes.

If only Papa didn't look so foolish when he talks that medicine talk, John thought. *Or if only I could just believe it all. Swallow it all.*

He lay that way for a long time as the storm approached. Then he heard the tearing sound of hard steady rain. It came as a curtain, sharp coolness before it, and John didn't care whether it soaked him or not.

Grandfather Rattlesnake

The weeks became months, and John heard nothing from his father. Sometimes Sedie Jumper, his cousin who ran the little store by the air-boat dock, came to visit, and once she brought John a letter from his mother. It was just a note, with a clipping from the tribal newspaper, about a woman from an Alaskan tribe who had come through, visiting. She had given a talk at the youth center, telling about the history of alcohol and Native Americans, and she had finished up with saying, "For one of us to stay sober is a revolutionary act." That was her message, and it was Anna's, too. John had expected a long letter saying how much she missed him.

After that, he began to really wonder how long they might leave him in the swamp.

Then one day Sedie came by to say Moses would be out to the res the next afternoon; he wanted John to meet him at the store.

"You want me to come and get you?" she asked John.

"No!" Mary said. "We don't need that air boat out here again tomorrow. He can take the canoe in."

They looked at John, as if to test him.

"Sure," he said. "I don't care."

He tried not to think about seeing his father, and he got away by himself as soon as he could. It was hard to get to sleep that night. After midnight a storm blew in, and it rained for hours, on into the morning. John waited it out, with nothing but worry on his mind. When it finally slacked off and quit, he still couldn't figure out how he would feel when he actually set eyes on Papa again. And he wondered, *Is this it? Is he going to bring me home with him now?*

It seemed years later when John finally eased the long dugout canoe into the weedy bank behind Sedie's little store. His father's air boat was in the willows, and John's stomach turned in anticipation.

An old refrigerator lay on its back with its door gone, and inside a big gopher turtle crawled in a slow circle; it would be Sedie's supper tonight. John walked into the rear of the store, where the air was still and tense. Silently, Sedie handed him a soda and a Twinkie, and her eyes told him not to speak.

Moses Raincrow stood by the broken jukebox with his powerful arms crossed and his wide, serious face focused on the man he was talking to. Moses nodded at his son and returned to his conversation, and John saw at once why he was so formal. The tall, bony white man in the khaki uniform, standing with his back to John, was Mr. Crane. He had red hair and thickly spread freckles over his skin, and not much humor about him at all.

"We know they're in the area," he said. "Don't try to fool me about that."

A dark blush of anger passed across Moses' face, and he looked out the open front door toward the old highway that cut through the reservation.

"We have a pretty good idea you could help us on this pair, Mr. Raincrow."

"Look," Moses said quickly. "I just got here. I been working all week on a gladiola farm. How do you expect me to know where two panthers are in this whole swamp, huh? Even if I knew last week— you think they haven't moved since I was out here? You think panthers don't move?"

Sedie Jumper began to laugh. John started in, too, then finally Moses. All of them together made a soft, musical sound. Even Mr. Crane closed his eyes and smiled.

"All right, Mr. Raincrow. You got me there," he said. "But you could help me look around, couldn't you? You could save me a lot of time."

Moses turned to his son and with a straight face said, "John, this is Mr. Ron Crane, of the state's Task Force. You ever met him before?"

"No!" Crane said loudly, reaching for John's hand over the counter.

"My son," Moses said. Crane pumped John's hand up and down.

John had been about to say yes, he had met this

man at school last year, when Crane had come to talk about saving the panthers because they were an endangered species. How could the man not remember him?

"He's a fine boy!" Crane said, releasing his hand. *How does he know if I'm fine?* John wondered.

Moses gazed out the door.

"Look," Crane said, "the pair I'm after . . . the big male's radio collar has gone dead on us. Shoulda been good another six months. Anyway, they were seen crossing the road up by Blackwater Creek, just last night. Heading east. 'Course, rain's washed out all their tracks by now. That's why I need you. Everybody out here, when I ask them, they say wait till you come. Ask you. So, I'm asking."

Moses glanced at Crane and returned to studying the palm trees beside the roadway.

"*Well?*" Crane said in exasperation.

Moses turned to him, jarred and frowning.

"Are you going to help me or not?"

Moses said quietly, "I don't know where those two panthers went, Mr. Crane. But if I did, I wouldn't tell you."

Now Crane stiffened up. "You know, sir, it's not *me* personally that's benefiting from all this work. Whatever you do . . . whatever effort you put yourself to . . . it's for the good of the animals out there."

"Oh?" Moses whispered.

"*Yes!*" Crane continued. "Do you think I *like* tracking panthers through this swamp? Do you

think I *enjoy* climbing up in trees and lowering them
to the ground? You may not know what this is all
about, Mr. Raincrow, but someday your children
might. This boy here"—he pointed directly into
John's face—"he might appreciate it some day.
There's only thirty of them left, Mr. Raincrow.
Thirty. This boy's children might thank you someday for what you did—away back when he was
young. It's like I tell the schoolchildren when I give
programs, this is really important! *You* can make
a difference! This is the hunt of a lifetime!"

Moses and Sedie and John were all turned away
from the loud white man. Then there was the sound
of tires in gravel out front, and they saw Max Poor
Bear's camo-painted jeep pulling in. His tape deck
was turned up loud, playing the Rolling Stones.

"Here's your man to help you!" Moses said, moving for the door. "Come on, son." They left Crane
with his hands in his pockets and walked out the
door. Max was leaning against his jeep, smiling.

"Look here!" Max said. "Moses and John together. Don't see that every day, now!"

"Hello," Moses said. "What are you doing out
here?"

"Come out to the swamp, man. Get away from
the Trail for a night. What else, huh?" Max laughed.
His big semiautomatic rifle lay on the seat of his
jeep. And beneath the roll bar, in the back, there
was a washtub loaded with ice and beer.

Moses looked glum, nodding. "You're out here

to get drunk and then go spotlighting. You'll shoot a few deer, and if the heat doesn't spoil them, you'll sell them in Miami. Am I right?"

"What an imagination," Max said.

"It's thanks to you," Moses said, "that the tribal council may have to pass some hunting laws."

"I'm scared to death," Max said lightly, smiling at John. "Whatever you boys are up to," Max said as he stepped away from his jeep, "best of luck to you."

He headed into the store, and Moses got into his pickup and crashed the door shut.

They pulled out and started down the road, neither wanting to talk about Max. They had driven only half a mile and John was about to ask where they were going, when they saw a small crowd in the schoolyard. The children and Ellen Cypress, their teacher, were standing close together, pointing at something, and they began to wave Moses down.

John could see the rattlesnake beside the soft pine stump on the grass as he opened his door.

"It won't go away!" one of the children cried out. Others laughed, and they all squeezed together.

"It's an old one," Moses said, easing close to the snake. It was about six feet long, thick, with the sharp black diamondback pattern, and it had a lot of rattles. "Does it live in there?" He pointed to the stump.

Ellen nodded. "It's been coming out every day." She spoke with deliberate calmness. "The children and I have been talking to it, haven't we, children?"

"Yes, Ellen!" they said. "But it doesn't listen."

"No," she agreed. "Any ideas, Moses?"

He squatted near the snake's head and said nothing. John knew he was trying to tune into it, setting the tone for a talk. Slowly, he took a little pouch of tobacco from his shirt pocket, worked a pinch of it between his thumb and forefinger, and sprinkled it on the ground beside the snake.

"Grandfather," Moses said to it, "we don't want to harm you, you know that."

The snake backed up a little; it was very sluggish.

"But each day you insist on coming out of your hole, and being near the children." He paused and looked at the sky, a clean blue with scattered white clouds.

"Now...that's no good. You might hurt one of them, even though you don't mean to."

Moses cocked his head and looked closely at the rattlesnake.

Then he stood up and faced the children, who were perfectly quiet, their dark eyes very round and wide. "I'm afraid there's something wrong with our friend," he said. "I believe he's very old, maybe sick, and it's time we sent his soul on its way."

There was a sound of the children drawing their breaths.

"Now, I know Ellen is a good teacher, and she's spoken to you about the souls of four-leggeds." They nodded. "And you know that the old people, going far, far back into time, they never would kill a rattlesnake. They didn't want his shadow after them!"

"*No!*" the children said.

"Of course not. And they especially didn't want the Sky Rattlesnakes mad at them, did they?"

"*Noooooooooo!*"

"That's right. Because if that happened, then next time you went anywhere—out for a walk, over to the store—anywhere you pick up your foot, you're going to put it down on a... what?"

"*Rattlesnake!*" they cried together. "*Rattlesnake!*"

"Shhhhh..." Moses glanced at the snake, moving off toward its stump hole. "That's right, children. But let's not yell." He picked up a stick from the grass and blocked the snake's way.

"That's why, every fall at the Hunt Dance, we always do the Snake Dance, don't we?"

"Yesssss!" they hissed together.

"Uh-huh. We always do that dance... to let the Sky Rattlesnakes know we mean no harm to the great tribe of snakes. No harm at all."

The big snake began to coil up.

"Our grandfathers, in the old days of our tribe, they knew better than to get the spirits mad at them ... they were pretty smart. Do you know what they did in a case like this, when a snake needed to be sent on to the other world?"

"*Nooooo,*" the children whispered, shaking their heads.

"Well, they went out and got a white man to kill it for them! That's right! If they could find one. Because he doesn't believe in the Sky Rattlesnakes, did you know that?"

Some of them nodded their heads, some shook them. John knew that they agreed, that they were listening to their medicine man.

"Well, we're lucky today," Moses said. "Because we've got John here with us." He looked up and smiled. "And John, the keys are in the truck. Do you think you could find us a white man, right quick?"

John turned to the children with the most worried face he could manage.

"I'll see what I can do," he said. "I'll go look for one."

"Good," Moses said. "You will be the medicine man's ceremonial assistant in this matter. While you find us a white man, who knows nothing of the snake's shadow or its master spirits up above, we will make our apologies to this Grandfather. Are you with me, children?"

"*Yessssssss!*" they cried, studying the snake for a sign that he understood, too.

John drove off in the pickup and returned within a few minutes, followed by Crane in his government truck and Max Poor Bear in his jeep.

"Hello, ma'am," Crane said to Ellen Cypress. "The boy here says you've got a rattler bothering these children—is that so?"

"Yes," she said, holding back a smile. She pointed to the coiled snake.

"Good night!" Crane said. "Look at the size of him. Get back everybody!" He got his revolver from his truck and stood very importantly over the snake.

Moses had moved away to the school's doorway and waited with his arms crossed, amused.

Crane started shooting with his .38 Special, and the snake made a half-hearted strike in his direction, falling just short of the man's leather boot. Crane yelled something at the rattlesnake and fired five more quick shots, two of which actually hit their target and finished it off.

"*Sheeehew!*" Crane said, wiping his forehead with the back of his revolver hand. "That was a bad one! Did you see how he came for me?"

He turned to the children and their teacher, then to John. But everybody was watching the dead rattlesnake, and none of them said a word.

Crane put his handgun away. He seemed a little shaken. "Good thing you came and got me," he called out to John. "That one there was deadly!"

"Thank you, Mr. Crane," John said.

"Don't mention it!"

The white man climbed into his truck, waved at everybody, and drove away.

Max Poor Bear put his arm around John's neck and pulled him to his side.

"Come with me tonight, cousin, and we'll kill four hundred frogs!"

"No thanks, Max."

"I'll split the cash with you."

"Where were you all this time, man?"

"Water under the bridge, little buddy. The important thing is, I'm out here now. I got you a taste of something nice, too." He tightened his arm around John's neck, bending him sharply over. "Whaddya say to that, huh?"

"Let me up, Max."

"You gonna come out with us and shoot deer tonight?"

"Just let me go, creep!"

"Hold it! Hold it right there, kid. You owe me money, and I'm offering you a chance to get even. Listen, that guy Crane? I know where those panthers like to lay up. I told him where to run his dogs in the morning, and he's gonna do it. Now, that'll set us up with the best deer drive you ever saw! Get me? He's gonna run everything in those thickets right out on top of us! And I know *exactly* where we need to be. You listenin', cuz?"

"You're chokin' me, man!"

Suddenly Max let him go. As John coughed and drew his fist, he saw that Max was paying no attention but was staring across the yard at Moses and the children.

"What's that?" Max asked. "What's he doin' now?"

Moses had draped the long broken body of the snake over the pine stump, and he was leading the children in a chanted apology to its shadow spirit and to the Sky Spirits of all rattlesnakes.

"Is he kidding?"

"No, 'course not, Max. He's teaching them."

Max watched in silence, rubbing his palms up

and down on his jeans. All at once he pulled a can of beer from the tub of ice in his jeep, popped it open as loudly as he could, and drank with the foam pouring out over his hand. He climbed in and drove away without a word.

Father and Son

John found himself with strange feelings toward his father as they left the little school. It was good to see him, that was the strongest sensation, and he wished his mother was out here, too. He was still angry about the way Moses had dragged him from home. But it was important now to prove he was strong—he had taken the harshness of the swamp and been just fine. He would show Papa how tough he was and also that he really didn't need drugs or alcohol at all. He wanted them again, as soon as possible, but nobody had to know that.

They drove down the blacktop road through the dense summer green of the glades, and Moses talked about why he had come to the reservation. It was to heal a few of the old people who had sent for him, and he hoped John would serve as his assistant, his medicine helper.

John listened and nodded. He didn't want to do it, but until this moment he would have been embarrassed by his father's request. Now, after seeing

Papa in action with that snake, he almost had to admire the old man for what he was trying to accomplish out here. There was no mention of the trouble between them, nor of Moses' plans for him. *Fine*, John thought, *let it alone for now. But don't think you're going to leave me out here again.*

They stopped at several houses while Moses talked and diagnosed at length, and finally he made arrangements to come back next weekend and perform the lengthy ceremonies. It was all a bit tedious for John, who wasn't sure what he was supposed to do, and also because he knew that everybody on the res had heard about his troubles. They would never say anything or ask questions, but their eyes were watching.

Finally the long afternoon came to its close. They drove up the winding wet road, spotted with puddles shining pink from the reflected sky, and Moses steered all over to avoid armadillos and rabbits. They seemed tame and curious, sniffing the world just before them.

"Mary been complaining about me?" Moses asked.

John smiled and told him about her deer sickness.

Moses nodded. "I know what she wants, son," he said. "I hope I can give it. But I can't spend days and days out there. And that's what it takes, really ...if you want to do the full treatment...if you want to be safe."

"Safe?"

"Sure. Try everything. Deer songs, rabbit songs,

maybe the horse songs, too. That stuff I can handle this time—if you help me. But when she starts up about her soul wandering ... and wants *those* old songs ... that's a lot more complicated. Takes time. I can't just snap my fingers and dance around the fire like some witch doctor in a movie!"

They laughed together. It was good to be alone with his father. It was better when nobody was around.

"A couple of times," John said, "Mary talked like her troubles could be sorcery."

Moses raised one eyebrow and closed the eye beneath it. "Ahhhhh. Who knows? I don't think so. Has she got any enemies *you* know of?"

"No."

"Me either. I doubt if anybody even knows those old spells anymore."

John leaned forward and caught his father's eye.

"I mean *almost* anybody!" Moses said.

And John wasn't so sure, suddenly, as they laughed again, that his father couldn't really burn souls, or cause sickness, or make lightning strike an enemy's camp, just as the old-time medicine workers claimed they could do.

Moses hit the brakes and they skidded to a sideways stop on the wet asphalt. A long slender blacksnake lay in a wiggly line ahead of them, nearly invisible in the fading light. Moses cut the engine, and the two of them sat in silence with the pickup blocking the road.

Moses breathed out a long sigh and rested his big head against his arms on the wheel.

"I'm tired," he said.

"I'll bet you are. So am I."

"Did you eat today?" Moses asked.

They faced each other in the darkness.

"Just a few bites of bass, early this morning."

"Good," Moses said.

"Why is that?"

"Look, Grandmother Mary's likely got the deer sickness and maybe some other problems along that line, too. I'm not saying it *couldn't* be sorcery, but this is what I think. The first thing, she's got to have some herbs and some songs—that's no problem. But she's also got to have soup tomorrow, made from the fresh backbone of a deer."

Moses waited a moment.

"Oh?" John said finally.

"Yes. If it's deer sickness, she's got to have it. And she can't eat any other fresh venison for months to come."

"I see."

"That's where I need you, son. I brought my .270 up—it's behind the seat in its case—and I want you to kill us a buck in the morning."

"In the morning?"

"Uh-huh. And not just any deer. There's a special old buck who lives in the Green Thicket. You remember?"

"Yes." John's throat was dry.

"Well, he probably stays there all the time, except for getting run out by dogs now and then."

"Oh."

"I need him for another reason, son. Not just for Mary's soup—any deer would do for that. But did you see, last summer, the shape our medicine bundle is in?"

"Yes, Papa. Mary told me all this."

"Oh. Well, that's fine. The hair's gone from half that bundle skin. We've got to have a buck with strong medicine of his own for a new one."

John just nodded.

"Good. Good. That's the biggest old buck I've seen or heard about on the whole reservation for a long, long time. I want you to kill him in the morning, for your great-grandmother, and for all the people, for their medicine pack."

"That's why you're glad I didn't eat?"

"Yes. We have to fast for the deer. We have to do this the right way. It's not an ordinary hunt."

"Sure. Of course."

Moses arched his back in a long stretch and reached for the key in the ignition.

"Let's get on out to camp," he said. "We've got a lot to do yet."

ΔΔΔ They drove to Sedie's store, walked down the bank, and climbed aboard the air boat that Moses had put together himself. John agreed with

Grandmother Mary about the noise and fumes, but he loved the flying ride over the swamp. Moses cranked up, and soon they were roaring down the flat canal, the wind tearing at their faces. John closed his eyes and drank it in. He tried to just feel the thrill of it, think of nothing, but he kept picturing the old buck. They had jumped him two years ago out of a cane patch beside a slough, and he was no more than twenty yards from them when he broke cover and sailed over a log into a shaft of sunlight, his great rack yellow and clean, frozen for John's memory in that instant of the leap.

As he thought of the buck, he imagined a strange whistling sound that seemed important, the way a song could remind him of a certain feeling. He focused on it against the whine of the air boat's engine, hearing it clearly inside his head: a soft whistle like nothing else he knew. Where had he heard it? And what was it connected to? Surely not the buck.

In a little while Moses cut the engine, and they drifted into the sawgrass channel of Mary's island.

When they reached her camp she was sitting up, stirring a stew made from alligator garfish, and she was smiling. It was very dark now, and she had built up the star fire. John wondered for a flash whether she was really as sick as she had seemed.

"Hello, Grandmother," Moses said, joining her on the log.

"Here at last," she said.

"John tells me you have the deer sickness."

She nodded and held her arm. She presented him

with a detailed accounting of her pains, mentioning each attack of spasms and cramps, and finally she retold her dreams about the deer.

"Living deer, dead deer, Sky Deer ... it's them, isn't it?"

Moses was leaning forward, studying the fire. "Maybe," he said quietly.

"*Maybe?*"

"If it is, we'll see what we can do for it."

"Oh, we will? How long are you here for?"

"Until late tomorrow, Grandmother. That's all I can stay. Now, listen to me. At daybreak, I'll go out and get the herbs and plants for your medicine. John knows what to do."

They both turned to him, and he was suddenly sure they had planned this together. But he wasn't sure, either. He was exhausted from the long day without food, and he didn't care anymore what they wanted—he would do it.

"Right now," Moses said, "John and I had better prepare the sweat."

She nodded, pleased. "You're going to find a surprise down there," she said.

Moses led his son into the dark and dripping palm woods, down the old path to the sweat lodge. And he was very happy with the new structure John had made. It seemed to lift him and give him energy. Together they carried the canvas, with a smoke hole in the center, to cover it over. Inside, they placed two short sitting logs, facing each other, with space left between them for the fire. Moses produced matches and a sealed bag of dry grass, pine shavings, and twigs. Beside the hut and covered over with palmetto fronds was a carefully stacked woodpile; it would be damp now, but with the start from the bag Moses could manage it.

Soon the blaze was licking through the popping sticks, and smoke was pouring up and out the hole. John and his father took off their clothes. John sat down, holding out his palms to the warmth. It wouldn't be long before he'd be roasting. His whole body would be slick with sweat, and he'd be too weak to walk to his sleeping platform in the chickee.

When the hut was so hot and dry that it hurt John's nasal passages to breathe, Moses brought his special pumice stones into the lodge and placed them on the fire. They heated up quickly, and they would retain their heat for a long time. Finally, Moses threw the first bucket of water onto the hot stones. They hissed like living things as steam exploded off them, and in an instant the air was breathable, and John's skin was getting wet. He and his father sat across from each other. This first part of the sweat was always best, before the steam became unbearable.

As they sat in silence and the steam boiled around them, John remembered how it was to do this years ago. *It was always like soft buckskin between us,* John thought.

"You know," he said, "it was strange the way Max acted about that rattlesnake today."

"Oh? How was that?"

"It upset him when you taught the children about the spirit and the Sky Rattlesnakes. Or it seemed to."

Moses nodded.

"You're not surprised?"

"Not really. You think about how Max lives. He doesn't care about the animal spirits. He kills deer like a white man."

"Sedie told me that last winter, when they had their season, it sounded just like a war across the north line," John said.

"That's it. They only get to hunt one little week in the year, so they think they have to kill everything that moves during that time."

"I'm glad we don't have seasons out here."

"We've always made our own seasons, son. When we need meat, then it's season. When we need medicine, season. The old grandfathers used to say that any man who kills without a need for it ... it's like with the snake ... he'll get his bite one day. If he wastes the deer, maybe he'll get the deer sickness."

"Max doesn't look sick yet."

They laughed together.

"No, he doesn't."

"Papa, do you think that old medicine—of the spirits getting mad enough to take revenge on two-leggeds—do you really think it's alive or dead?"

Moses started to answer and then hesitated. *He*

must be glad to get a question like this from me, John thought. *But he doesn't want to give me some line I'm supposed to believe.*

"All I know," Moses finally answered in a quiet voice, "is that we can't lose our faith, son."

"No."

"No, we can't. We can't start treating the world like the white man does."

"Like Crane."

"Yes," Moses said, annoyed, "like Crane. He means well, I think, within his lights. He wants to save the panthers. But look at the way he does it. Runs them with dogs, shoots them with those tranquilizers, locks radio collars on them ... and what happens when they die from that treatment? Nothing."

John nodded.

Moses got up and poured a second bucket onto the rocks. The steam rose up, hissing, and filled the lodge.

"He's an ignorant man, son. The whites came into this country long ago, and we showed them the panther. So they killed him for his fur, to make coats for their women and belts for the men. And finally they built highways right through the heart of his country. So now, the white man's cars go speeding down through there and kill the few that are left."

They sat together without talking then. After a while the steam was gone, and Moses poured another bucket of cold water onto the pumice stones.

"Now, Max," Moses finally said, "he's a little different from Crane. Max enjoys his killing. He uses that .458 Winchester Magnum, a rifle that's perfect if you're in Alaska hunting bear or elk ... but it's too big for our deer. It's just a show thing with Max and his buddies. The blast and the kick are terrible."

"He says he can kill more deer with it."

"He does, huh? Well, that's right. But so what? How many does he need to kill?"

"He is selling them, like you suspected."

"Uh-huh."

John nodded. He was feeling very weak and light-headed, but he didn't want this time with his father to end. It was so strange to be talking about Max. *But Papa cares more about me than Max ever did*, John thought.

"In a way," Moses said, "Max is the Indian who's taken on Crane's way of seeing. Here he is with that big rifle and his jeep, and now he's more dangerous than Crane is. But that Crane makes me mad! Did you hear him lecturing me?"

"Yes."

"Ohhhhh!"

"Papa," John said, "Grandmother Mary keeps talking about you getting a panther skin and claws. She says if you're going to help her with the deer sickness and the rabbit sickness, you've got to scratch her and scare off the deer spirits with the claws."

"I know, I know."

"Maybe you'll get one from that place in Montana?"

Moses jerked his head up. "Hah!" he said. He moved to the sweat-lodge door and reached out for his jeans. From a hip pocket he pulled out a small, wrinkled-up letter. "This is from them!" he said. "A thousand dollars, John. They want a thousand dollars for a panther skin!'"

"Oh."

"No way I can afford that."

"No."

Moses threw the letter into the fire, and they watched it curl and burn.

"Here the white man kills panthers for sport, and he kills them with his highways, and he kills them trying to help them. And the old Indian, who just needs *one* for his medicine, he won't do it because there're so few of them left."

Moses shook his big fist at the fire. His eyes were lost in the steam and the smoke.

"There're plenty of deer," John said.

"What? Oh, yes. But that doesn't mean Max needs to go slaughtering them and selling them in Miami. We don't have *that* many deer."

"No ... "

"Are you thinking about the old buck?" Moses asked.

"Yes ... "

"Hate to shoot him?"

John looked straight into his father's eyes across the fire and nodded his head.

"That's good, son. That's how you should feel."

"It is?"

"Yes. We need that buck. And you've fasted for him, and now you've taken your sweat to purify yourself for him. Soon you'll lie down and dream. If you're supposed to kill him tomorrow, you'll have the Hunt Dream, telling you where he is."

"Yes."

"That's right. And then, if it's supposed to be, the buck will come to you. He'll be the first thing you'll see, and he'll make his Give Away to you."

"I know."

"Then you'll bring him back, and he'll be your Give Away to Grandmother Mary and to the medicine bundle."

"I understand, Papa."

"So it's not like Max's killing in any way, son. And I'm proud of you when you tell me you won't enjoy doing it."

John nodded slightly. *I'll hate to shoot him,* he thought, *but I want to shoot him, too.*

They sat together through the steam of one more bucket, and then they walked down to the canal and bathed in the cool water.

When John finally lay to rest in the chickee he was limp and empty, and his mind felt free. He was ready to receive the Hunt Dream.

The Hunt Dream

John came up straight out of his dream. Moses'
hand was on his shoulder in the darkness, he was
trembling, and there was dripping . . . the same slow
dripping as in the dream about the deer. He licked
his lips and listened, felt his heart racing. The deer
were running across wet green pasture, their bright
tails bouncing, making quick strokes in the air. They
were jumping over logs, racing for the pine timber
ahead . . . a big panther was in among them! He
dodged back and forth, snatching for one, raking
a hindquarter, snapping at a neck. . . . Then they
were swallowed up by the black shadows of the
woods.

The panther stood fooled, frustrated, on the open
grass, jerking his long crooked tail in an angry
switch. Then he walked slowly, almost daintily, into
the thickety gloom.

"Son?"

"Oh. Yeah."

"Awake?"

"Sure."

"Still in the dream?"

John nodded. His father rose and tended the fire. In a moment John stood on his feet, tested his movements... he was so light, empty, still weak... and his heart was going like the heart of a bird.

He slid the rifle from its soft case. Its shoulder strap had a few loops and contained four cartridges. For a moment he stood in the dark with it slung, heavy, over his right shoulder, and he watched his father's outline against the fire.

He felt his father's awareness, and his investment of hope.

"I'll see you by noon," John said.

"Good. Be careful."

"I will."

All the words had been said. He headed down the trail in the pitch darkness, knowing each step and each turn, moving quickly to be past any scorpions or snakes before they had time to react. When he reached the sawgrass he heard a big alligator slide across in front of him and splash into the marshy mud, leaving a wake of popping air bubbles on the surface. In the blackness a crow gave a single cry.

Then John was poling the cypress canoe, easing up the canal, tasting the air for a direction of the uneven breeze. It would take him thirty-five minutes to reach his turn, then another fifteen minutes on a small creek. From there he would have the slightest gray of predawn to walk by, which was good because last week, when he was over in this area, he'd discovered a family of coral snakes living near his path.

It was fine to be alone on the canal, the air chilled, a layer of fog and mist hanging in ragged patterns between the lush banks. Dim forms of palms and pines began to hang over the water, and the surface became metallic instead of black. A pair of alarmed ducks quacked to each other with low croaking sounds and swam rapidly around a bend up ahead. In a while everything was visible, and the canoe was poking into the weeds where he would leave it.

He walked across the cutover pines near the water, then entered a dense woods of tall cabbage palms above and thickly jammed spiky yucca below. Very carefully he threaded his way along, until on the far side a clear flat pasture stretched away for half a mile. Beyond it lay the Green Thicket, where his father had said the buck might still be. Standing in the early light and looking over the field, John thought he recognized the scene from his dream. *Was it really a Hunt Dream? A true prophecy of where the buck will be today?* But it wasn't a dream of the old buck, at least not the part he woke up with.

John studied the long expanse of grass, waiting for movement. More than halfway to the distant woods, a single yellow pine grew wide and bushy, its limbs spread low and heavy from the open sun. John hurried to it and climbed up easily to a height of ten feet above the ground. He sat on one limb with his feet resting comfortably on another, and he had a window to watch and shoot through. It was almost as good as having a platform—the kind of tree stand Max was always putting up and bragging about.

The pine smelled good, and he was glad for his perch as the minutes began to slide. The sky was a fine silvery skin, glowing from inside. Out before him a thin layer of rainwater lay in the grass, and a huge flock of blackbirds came floating in to feed and talk there. They sounded like musical hinges on an old door, with their incessant skreeing and skrawking. As suddenly as they had come, they rose in a thunder wind and folded upon themselves in a graceful cone, flying away. John was dazed by hunger and tiredness, hypnotized by their motion within their black flock-cloud, and he slowly turned his head to see what had frightened them. It stood in the open pasture, switching its long tail, the tail from the dream.

At first it seemed a tawny doe, hornless and low to the earth. But it wore that wrong tail, a cat's tail, and then he saw what it really was. The panther cocked its head at the vanishing blackbirds, as if curious or amused. Then it sat down suddenly, its hind legs folded and its front legs straight, and it curled its tail around its body and licked its lips with its long tongue. John grinned. He had a perfect sight through the thick branches that covered him. A loud, whining mosquito flew into his ear and lit there, and he waited while it tickled him and made its stinging bite. He couldn't move except to wiggle his ear in vain. But it was worth being bitten by a whole cloud of mosquitoes to see this cat. It stood up again, looked in all directions for an instant, then ran in long, loping strides to the safety of the woods.

John smiled grandly now and slapped the mosquito. He might not see any deer today, but he sure would bring back a story. It was the first time he'd ever seen a panther. *What about that dream?* he thought. The panther would probably scare all the deer out of the Green Thicket for this morning. John resettled himself and decided to think it out. He had dreamed this place and the panther running. *But what about the deer with their white tails? Maybe they were just crazy dream deer, in there because of all the talk last night.* But it amazed him that he seemed to have had a genuine Hunt Dream. *If that much of the hunting magic is true,* he thought, *then what about the Give Away? Surely the panther didn't mean to give himself to me. . . . It was an easy shot . . . I could have raised the rifle without his seeing . . . but Papa didn't ask me to kill him a cat!*

John stayed in the pine for another hour. He had just about decided to come down and stretch and take a little walk, when he heard hounds strike a scent down at the west end of the woods, nearly two miles away. They were big-chested dogs with deep, steady voices, with rising tones that harmonized and then clashed and finally leveled out on a high, energetic chord. *Crane's dogs,* John thought.

Max led him here, and Max was right about the cat. The hounds were coming toward John, working slowly in the tangled brush and sharp spikes of the swamp. *If the panther went back that way, then they might run him out again.*

John twisted his head back and forth in the thick pine needles to get the best view. The dogs were steady and strong, patiently suffering their way up the long island of undergrowth. *Whatever is in there this morning is going to run out,* John thought. *No telling what I might see.*

Then the shots rang. They were straight ahead in the woods, less than half a mile from the first trees. Three loud, unbelievably loud shots shattering the quiet of the field. *It has to be the .458 Magnum,* John thought, *the rifle too big for the deer. It has to be Max.*

AAAAAAAAAAAAAAAAAAAAAA **9**

Last Morning

The male panther had lain with his mate in the hour before dawn. They had been warm and still in the leaves beneath a fallen oak top, its dry crackly branches tangled with briers. They would have heard anything approaching. Their stomachs were full from the boar they had run and caught together in last evening's dusk, and as they slept their tails twitched, their tongues moving when they dreamed.

The male traveled his territory alone most of the year, sharing the hunt and the warmth of a female only on the rare occasions when they met during her estrus. Then they struck a companionship that would last two weeks. Already they had mated many times, and she carried the first dividing cells of next season's cubs inside her body. The panther opened his eyes in the dawn and watched her face.

Off in the swamp a deer coughed. The panther's ears went up, and he blinked the sleep from his sticky eyelids as he listened. There was the *stamp, stamp* of the deer's delicate hoofs on the ground, another sharp, coughing bark, then the crashing into brush as two of them rapidly faded away. They either smelled him or were frightened by something else. The panthers didn't stir. They had plenty of hog left for their next meal. There was no need to rush anywhere.

The female breathed deeply and the male returned his attention to her. The last time he had met another panther, it was on the savannah beyond the three marshes. It was near the hard, black trail where the things with lights and noise roared by. That panther was a young male and the older one had known it from the first irritating whiff. A single, quick growl was the only warning he gave before he took two leaps and sprang onto the other cat's back, raking the hide from his ribs and trying for the deathbite on his wide, hard neck. But the younger one had torn himself free and vanished like fog in the darkness. Just then a noise thing had come thundering straight down the black trail, and by the time it passed out of hearing and sight, the young panther's smell had almost faded away.

All at once the female was awake, licking her lips, and he heard her stomach growling.

They rose and sniffed each other and purred over each other's necks for a moment. Then they trotted out of the brushtop and headed down to the slough, where the hog was hidden. They had stashed it beneath branches, and it took only a moment to drag it free. Then they buried their faces in the strong, cool flesh once again, tearing it from the heavy body. Soon they were sitting facing each other, gnawing and worrying the white bones, cracking them and licking the yellow marrow inside.

As the fog began to rise on the marsh, the panthers abandoned their kill and moved slowly into the wind. They would need to feed again in a few hours, and this long tangled thicket might yield a deer, or at least a rabbit. Last week they had smelled a flock of turkeys here, too, and had managed to snag one on the ground before the others crashed noisily into the sky.

Moving up the edge of the woods, the male looked out from time to time into the open pasture unrolling away from him. Sometimes he had seen deer out there, especially at dawn and dusk, and he had often smelled them feeding at night. It was a calm morning, with no sound or smell to disturb him, and he left his mate and walked boldly out into the light.

He made his way across the bright field, walking on lightly flooded green grass, and when he reached a tiny island of dry ground, he sat down. Far off in the thicket he smelled a deer. Suddenly an enormous cloud of blackbirds came flying in and lit, spreading themselves out in a wide fan across the green. After a moment they rose before him, noisier than before, and took strange patterns as they flew toward the woods. It was as if they had blended into one great animal.

Alert and wary now, the male stood up and loped

to the trees. The shade and cover swallowed him
again, and he hurried through a kudzu mass toward
the female's scent.

For a long time they explored the foggy woods,
wandering for half a mile into the soft breeze, then
abruptly turning around and slipping back along
their own fresh tracks. They moved in a leisurely
pace, even playing a few times with paw swipes at
each other's heads, their claws safely retracted.

They were drinking from a shallow pool beneath
a gumbo limbo tree when they heard the dogs.

Of Science and Dogs

Ron Crane had his khaki pant leg caught in black-berry briers when his dogs cut loose. He yelled in surprise and jerked his foot free, tearing a line of thorns into his skin. *Here we go,* he thought, as he started to run. *Durn cats'll tree, like as not, before I can get through this stuff.* He faced the wall of brier and yucca ahead, sighed with discouragement, and plunged in.

He was a man determined to do his job. And his job was to tree a certain number of panthers every year, shoot them with the harmless tranquilizer gun, tattoo their ears with blue dye, weigh them and check their teeth while they were still groggy, and make sure their radio collars were transmitting just right.

It was a hot, thankless expense of energy, most of it done alone in this huge swamp. If he went down by himself in quicksand and was finished off by alligators or scorpions, it was possible that no-body would ever know. *People are suspicious of a government man,* he thought as he ran. *Always will be. Especially these Indians. They don't know who to trust—can't blame 'em for that—and they've got no idea about the science of wild animals.*

His dogs were howling louder and hotter, and he was fighting the thicket with both arms and thinking about his revolver. He'd never use it unless he had to, but with two cats at one time, you never could tell. If Max Poor Bear was right, this could be the pair he wanted.

He broke free of the mass of blackberry and ran faster, jumping with his long legs over yucca spikes and palmetto fronds, dodging the low black limbs of live oak trees. As he passed into their deep shadows, those powerful oak arms interlocked gracefully, their crooks and branchings lying just above him with the suggestion of waiting snakes. He ran harder. Clutching the dart rifle, he listened to the dogs, straining for every slight change in their direction.

He loved those dogs. Dottie was a redbone bitch with a pedigree out of Texas coonhound stock, and Sparky was a huge bluetick who looked classic but had no papers. They'd been trained by a famous lion man, as the western cougar-hunting guides were called, and the state had paid for them and for their trainer's time during the first two years. By then Crane had learned almost as much about them as the expert and had fallen for the thrill of working with them. He'd decided to buy them for himself.

What a great thing it is, Crane thought as he ran, *that science calls for this chase.* Crane was from western Kansas and he disliked Florida, the heat and bugs and snakes especially; but he liked his job. He even liked complaining about it. The panthers were down to the last thirty now. *A critically endangered species if there ever was one,* he thought as he ran on. *The cars on Alligator Alley kill them, and nobody knows how many the rednecks shoot. Nobody knows how many they get mounted by some sorry, crooked taxidermist, how many they nail up in secret on the walls of their camphouses and their dens.*

He stopped and wiped his face.

The government had waited mighty late in the cats' existence to get involved. But now they had seen fit to put Ron Crane on it, and with all his powers he would see it through. *Without knowledge of the cats,* he heard himself saying to classes of schoolchildren, *we'd never know how to manage them. Without the Texas lion dogs, and the radio collars, and the guns that shoot those knockout darts...why it'd just be your guess against mine about how many of them are left at all...about what they do...where they go...and, most important of all, about how to save them.*

The children were always thrilled. The Greatest Hunt in the World, was the title of Crane's lecture. *The panther just wants to be left alone,* he loved to tell them. *So do him a big favor, kids, and give him what he wants. If you see one, it'd be the best thing*

*of all if you'd keep it to yourself... don't tell a soul!
Do you think you could do that?*

Crane reached up and grabbed a low pine limb and hung there for a second, feeling his heart beat. His dart rifle was slippery with sweat, and its stock was scarred with bright new scratches. He felt the weight of the darts and serum in the green cloth pouch at his belt.

Max sure knows his cats, Crane thought. *Maybe that Raincrow had no idea where they'd be.... That's why he wouldn't help me... didn't want to lose face with his own.*

The dogs broke into an excited pitch, and Crane took off again.

More likely though, he thought, *he knew just as well. Everybody sure said he would. Ignorance. That's it, that's all it is. He's got no idea in this world what our project is about.*

Then the hounds treed. There was no sound on earth like that one, their long unbroken line of howling through the echoing trees suddenly brought to a fixed boiling point in the swamp. Crane pictured the cats aloft, nervous and snarling at his dogs, trying to decide whether to jump and run, or fight. Or would they simply wait, with their nervous stomachs and hearts? Crane was running around deadfalls and stumps now, oblivious of snakes and scorpions, focused only on his wonderful dogs— the soft fur of their throats, their tender-skinned loins and bellies. He had to get there before the panthers jumped.

The baying chorus was just beyond the next bog, and he had only to run wide around it, through a prickly thicket of cypress saplings, and all at once he saw both cats together, perched in a tall pine. They were on the same thick limb, switching their positions; their tails were long and stiff, then twitching and curling. Their teeth were bared over pink gums, against black muzzles, and their ears were flattened on their round heads. All their anger and energy was directed at the howling dogs.

Both Dottie and Sparky were stretched tall on the base of the pine, digging into the loose bark with their long front claws, muscles and ribs showing through their skin. They whined frantically as Crane broke through to them.

Crane was after the big male panther with the dead radio collar. But now he was shielded by the female, and they were twisting back and forth, on the brink of jumping. Crane opened the rifle's breech, took a dart syringe from his pouch, filled it with serum for the bigger cat's weight, and inserted it. He took quick aim.

Switch positions once more, he prayed. *Just once more.*

The cats glared through slitted eyes and spit at him. He lowered the rifle and took a few steps forward. It would be an easy shot now, if she would just move over. Sparky grabbed a thin sapling in his teeth and began tearing it back and forth, stripping its gray bark and slobbering, then shredding it into long, thin filaments. Both panthers jumped.

They were aiming for a lower limb on another pine, and they sailed together for an instant, as if in slow motion. They landed, struggling to hold on as the branch sprang up and down beneath their weight. In that moment he had a clear vision of the male's hind leg, and he fired the silent dart. The cats jerked away in unison and stared at him. He saw the long projectile hanging heavily from tan fur, and he grinned in satisfaction. He had done it again. But something was wrong. The neck of that panther showed no collar, and as he grasped this, the other cat leaped away from the back of the pine and was gone from sight. It landed deep in the tall grass and dry brown tops, and shot away with heavy bounds that quickly faded from hearing.

Crane couldn't believe what he had done. He stood there, wringing wet, mosquitoes singing around his ears, staring dumbly up at the female cat, who now seemed very calm. Her eyelids sagged. She surged once, awkwardly, and dug her claws into the meat of the pine. She licked her lips. In a moment she slid from the limb, hung beneath it, and breathed heavily. She closed her eyes and fell.

In the Spirit of Greed

From high in his pine tree, John heard the dogs stop barking. Then there was silence, and finally, very faintly and far away, he heard a buzzing whine. At first it was no more than the annoyance of a mosquito on the fringe of awareness, but then he detected a bass rumble inside the sound, and as it grew louder he knew it was a motor. It came closer in a weaving, broken pattern, revving up one moment and disappearing the next. He knew it was Max's three-wheeled motorcycle.

John began to climb down. *So he's killed something*, he thought, *and now he's coming to get it.* Max was an amazing shot with that rifle, often shooting two deer on the run in a single burst of fire. Then he would three-wheel them out of the swamp, into his truck, and sell them in Miami before the meat spoiled. Max could make good money at it, but that wasn't his reason for the energy he put into the work. It's those big, warm animals, Moses had said. There's something about killing deer that brings out the blood lust in a lot of men, son.

Slowly, John walked across the open field and entered the woods. He moved toward the remembered sound of the shots, and he knew the three-wheeler was headed to the same spot from the far side. Soon it shut off.

He slipped quietly through the dark cypresses, careful to step in wet leaves and avoid sticks. The last thing he needed was for Max to think another deer was coming toward him.

John had another two hundred yards to go. He listened, waited, and slowly closed the distance. Soon he saw Max tying the heads of the deer to the back of his red machine.

"Ho!" John called.

Max jerked up and reached for his rifle, against a tree.

John waved.

"Oh," Max said in a moment. "Well, I'll be."

John walked on in, and there were two does tied up and ready to drag.

"Max strikes again, huh?"

"You bet," he grinned. "Want a beer?" He pulled one from the six-pack that dangled from his handlebars.

"No, thanks."

"You deer hunting?" Max asked.

"Uh, yeah. Didn't see anything, though."

"Too bad. You should have come with me. I invited you, you know."

"Yeah. Guess I should have."

John looked at the stiffening does, their dull eyes glassy and gray. Their legs were twisted oddly beneath them.

"You don't dress them first?"

"Nope. Don't want to get their body cavities full of leaves and stuff. I'll do it at the truck."

"Oh." John knew that this was improper.

"I don't pray to the grandfather spirits, either," Max said.

"Well, watch out for deer sickness, then," John snapped, surprised at himself for standing up to his old friend.

"Deer sickness, huh?" Max took a long swallow from his can. "You buying that stuff now?" he said.

John looked away. Max had so much power about him, John always wanted to be on his side.

"Deer sickness," Max said, as if he were playing with the thought. "Look, the medicine people say that in the old times, when animals could talk to humans, they noticed that the humans were getting dangerous. They were killing too many of the four-leggeds. You know the story, right?"

"That's right."

"Uh-huh. So the four-leggeds stopped talking to the two-leggeds, and each one came up with a different disease to punish the two-leggeds."

John nodded.

"Yeah." Max grinned. "And if you only take what you need, and if you apologize to the animal spirits, and the Sky Spirits, and if you do the Hunt

Dances in the fall...do this, do that...have the right thoughts...are you with me?"

"Of course," John said sadly.

"Then the animals will leave you alone! Isn't that generous of them?"

John was studying the two deer.

"Well, son," Max continued, "I'm here to tell you that's bull. It's just Old Indian talk, is all it is. I don't apologize to nobody."

Max threw down his empty beer can in anger and tore another one from the plastic loops hanging from the three-wheeler.

"Max..."

"And I don't burn no ears and no tail, neither! Tell that to your medicine-man pappy!" He popped open his beer.

When John refused to argue, Max continued on his own. "Does that mean the deer can hear me next time? Does it mean they'll show me their tails when they run away? Somehow, I don't think these right here got the message...."

Max laughed, drank, studied John's eyes.

"Look," John said, "my father asked me to bring in a deer's fresh backbone so he can make soup for my great-grandmother this morning. It's part of the cure."

"She got the deer sickness?"

"He thinks so."

"There is no cure for deer sickness. He didn't tell you that?"

"Sometimes there is."

"Almost never. I'm just quoting what the old folks say. Anyway, you didn't get a deer, did you?"

"No. So how about if you let me have just a piece of the backbone of one of yours?"

"Oh! Now he wants *my* deer's backbone! He wouldn't take my offer of hunting with me. But now he wants me to give him a deer!"

"Just a piece, Max. I'm asking for Grandmother Mary."

Max stood looking, grinning. Then he drank from his can, picked up his rifle, walked over, and sat down on his three-wheeler.

"I'll tell you what, John. I could let you take what you want, here, and I'd have a real mess to drag back to my jeep. Now, if I believed in this witch doctor stuff, for the old lady's sake I might do it. But I want you to wake up, kid. There's no point in tearing up my deer for a shaman stew! Mary's an old, old woman, John. She's got arthritis and rheumatism."

John's lip and his left eyelid were trembling.

"But," Max said, "if you really feel you've got to have a deer..."

He set the switches on his three-wheeler, took hold of the starting cord, and gave a hard yank. It sputtered and then roared into life, pouring a stream of black exhaust into the weeds. "...then I suggest you get started hunting!"

With a final laugh, Max adjusted his sling over his back, hanging the scoped rifle across his chest, and took off fast over the woods floor. The two big deer slid easily behind him, leaving a wide, flat path of mud and hair to mark his trail.

John stood there, exhausted and murderously angry. The day was heating up now, and his knees were too weak to walk to the canoe. The rifle over his shoulder weighed on him like a great rock. He turned to go. He walked slowly, breathing deeply, trying to get Max out of his heart. At this moment, everything Max had said felt true. Maybe animals were just animals, and two-leggeds were just what they seemed, too. Maybe nothing mattered but having a good time. When he was with Max, it was so hard not to believe it.

All at once John saw a spot of bright red blood on the side of a little oak. Off to his right there was another drop, and another. From Max's deer? He followed the drops and they were leading away at a crazy angle into the brush. Max must have hit another one with that last shot. And not bothered to look for it.

The spots ran out after fifty yards.

Moses had taught him how to trail a wounded deer, and once had taken him on a hunt where they had to do it. John reached down into his shirt pocket and found a carefully folded square of orange plastic; then he took out his knife and cut off a piece and tied it to a branch by the last drop of blood. He set out to walk very slow circles, each one wider than the last, and he got down and crawled on his hands and knees at the sign of anything red. The minutes dragged by until it seemed as if hours were passing. The blood had simply run out.

Finally, in a last attempt, he tried walking a straight line from the final few spots on the trail.

He went quietly, his rifle ready in his hands, his thumb on the safety catch. High above in the trees, the first real wind of the day came in a gust, bending the tops with a loud, swooshing noise. Jaybirds flew up with sharp cries, and a big gray squirrel hopped across the leafy ground. The world seemed so vast, John would never find this wounded deer.

He took a few more steps.

Then he stopped again to rest, to grit his teeth at Max. If only Max were wrong about the animals. If only he could prove it.

The wind blew down over him with a sudden coolness, a few leaves danced, and patches of blue sky showed high above as the clouds broke up. The return of fair weather to the woods seemed to mark the end of this episode, to say that this search was hopeless. He was ready to quit.

Just a few more steps.

And there in the distance was the round, white belly of the deer.

John raised his rifle almost to his shoulder and put a little pressure on the safety catch. He walked toward the deer as quietly as he could, but he couldn't help hurrying.

It didn't move.

And in a moment he was standing over the body of a small dead buck.

His first thought was horror—this beautiful, sleek, gray-and-white animal, stretched out so lean and graceful in the leaves—it ought to get up, and breathe, and jump. It ought to run away, startled, into the trees. It was the same feeling he'd had when Moses took him on a hunt and killed one. Max's voice came playing through his head, laughing, saying, *We all die sometime, and when it's over it's over.*

But as he stood there staring at the creature, its small forked horns, its long smooth lines, John knew he needed it. *Maybe it'll help Grandmother get well,* he thought. *Maybe even Papa would accept this skin for the medicine bundle.* John was willing to kill the old buck if it was really necessary. Secretly, he'd thought he might be thrilled by doing it. But now it seemed he wouldn't have to. And looking at the still body on the earth before him, he knew he didn't want to do it.

He laid his rifle against a maple tree and spoke softly to the little deer's spirit.

"Grandfather, hear me. I didn't shoot you this morning. I only found you here in this place. Grandfather, we need this backbone, for healing, and we need this hide, for the medicine bundle. I'm sorry you had to die. Grandfather, I don't apologize for Max, and the way he did it. But I apologize for myself, because I'm going to dress this body, now, and spill this blood. Thank you, Grandfather, if this was your Give Away."

John was surprised at the ease of his prayer. He

had heard his father speak in such tones to animal spirits before, and he'd had thoughts like these, but this was the first time he had actually spoken them aloud.

And he felt something else new. Now that the buck had received his apology and his thanks, its body was no longer the place of its spirit. It was now meat. And he felt its spirit still here in the woods, surrounding them. John looked up at the gently swishing treetops bathed in sunlight. He turned slowly and studied the shady woods around him, seeing a small lizard watching him from a yucca, a wild canary flitting inside a button snake-root bush. He smelled the rich vegetable mud of the swamp floor. It was alive after all, *all of it*, he felt in a rush. Max was wrong about the woods and the animals.

Then John drew his old knife, wrapped long ago by his great-grandfather in the piece of alligator hide, and he began the work of dressing out the deer. He had helped his father once, and he had watched this done at the Green Corn Dance. He soon discovered that, without help, it was more work than he remembered.

Twenty minutes later the buck was cleaned out, steaming and slowly cooling, and John was washing his hands and arms in a clear rainwater pool. Then he walked back and stood surveying his work. The deer was too heavy for him to carry or drag out, especially in his weakened state. Even though he had brought a length of rope to hoist it into a tree, to keep it safe from predators until he and his father could return, he was sure he didn't have the strength.

He thanked the spirits that the woods had dried out so much, and he began to lay a little fire of twigs and grass. When it was burning well he turned to the buck. Reaching inside his body, John removed the tenderloins from where they were attached to the backbone, and he skewered them on a green oak stick. Then he roasted them over his fire.

"*Grandfather*," he whispered without thinking, "*thank you for this food now about to enter my body. As this buck was given away to me, so I'll give this strength to Grandmother Mary.*"

The tenderloins were delicious, and after eating them John smiled for the first time in a long while. Then he stretched out under a palm tree and drifted to the edge of sleep, letting the buck's strength become his own.

Finally he rose, refreshed. Now he would ritually burn the ears and tail, which would keep the deer from hearing him in the future, and from escaping with their tails flying behind. Or would that help Max, who was the actual killer of this deer? He wasn't sure, but he would do it anyway.

Then he would drag the buck to his canoe. It might take all afternoon, but he knew he would make it. He had the power of the warm meat inside him, and—unless he and his father were both crazy—the blessing of the deer's soul.

ΛΛΛΛΛΛΛΛΛΛΛΛΛΛΛΛΛΛΛΛΛΛΛ **12**

Humiliation

John made it to the island in the late afternoon. He told his story, and he knew his father was proud of what he had done. Together they hung the buck from a limb and carefully skinned it. Then Moses set John the task of cutting little cubes of meat for roasting and drying—this deer would feed Mary for a long time to come—and he began to make her special medicine soup. After this, she would be forbidden to eat fresh venison for four months, but the dried and smoked meat would be all right.

When the work was done, the peach and pink of sunset were beginning to glow across the clear sky. Moses and John lay down on sleeping platforms in the chickee, wordless and tired, each pleased with the part he had been able to play.

They were dreaming deeply when Grandmother Mary shook them awake.

"Get up!" she cried. "Get up and listen!"

They were dazed, trying to comprehend her strength, and then they realized what she was yelling about. A loud air boat had come up the canal and was sputtering to a stop by her entry creek.

"Who's that?" she cried, shaking John's shoulder with her old iron grip. *"Go see! Quick!"*

Sleepily, John and Moses stumbled from the chickee and headed down toward the water. They glanced at each other. "Great place to rest, huh?" Moses said.

A figure was emerging from the sawgrass and cane, and in a moment they recognized the thin form of Sedie Jumper.

"What are you doing, Sedie?" Moses said angrily. "You know how Mary hates the air boats to come up here. You could've at least drifted in the last few hundred yards."

"Listen," she said, holding up her hand for patience. "I've got something to tell you. You know that government man, Crane?"

"Yeah?"

"Well, he stopped by the store this afternoon, and guess what he had in the back of his truck?"

"The great horned snake," Moses said. "I don't know, Sedie. What?"

"A female panther. He killed her with that dart gun of his."

Moses' face tightened as he took it in.

"Where was he going with her?" he asked at last.

"I don't know. But he said something about the heat, and how he had to get her in the freezer."

"They've got a freezer in the back of their office," Moses said. "Thanks for coming out, Sedie."

"I wanted to come sooner, but I had the store by myself."

He nodded.

They all walked together up to the chickee. Moses was lost in his own thoughts. Sedie told Grandmother Mary about the panther.

"That's it!" she cried out. "That's the last bit of it that I can stand! They come out here saying they're going to save the panthers, and look what they do, Moses! There's your cat! Go get it for yourself, right now!"

"I was just thinking about that."

"Don't think, do it! Go tell them whose cat that is!"

Slowly, Moses turned to John.

"Would that panther's medicine work for you?" John asked quietly.

"I'm going," he said. "Want to come with me?"

"I sure do," John said.

▲▲▲ Moses drove his air boat hard through the swamp. When they reached the willows of the bank behind Sedie's store, he tied up fast, beside her own air boat, and they scrambled to his pickup truck.

Then he and John were traveling in the warm night down the narrow highway, silent and excited. John knew his father must be forming his words, trying to plan how he would talk to the white man. It was a shame, now, that he had refused to help them find the panthers. They might want to punish him by keeping the dead cat for themselves.

The Endangered Species Task Force field office was a simple, low-roofed building on the highway, twenty-two miles north of the reservation. Moses skidded to a stop in the gravel in front of it and set his emergency brake with a hard jerk. He slammed his door as if to warn them inside.

The building was brightly lit, and there were three trucks parked outside.

Moses hurried to the door and knocked. John was close behind him.

"Yes?" It was tall Crane, stooping slightly, peering at Moses in the yellow glare of the porch bulb.

"Hello, Mr. Crane," Moses said. "You remember me, don't you?"

"Uh..."

"And my son, John."

"Oh! Raincrow! Of course. I found those panthers without your help, you know. That Max must be as good as you are."

"I hear you killed one of them."

"Yeah, yeah, I hate to admit it, but I sure did. Caught her with the dose intended for the male. He's a lot bigger, you know. Pure accident, 'course. I feel lousy that it had to happen."

"Would you mind if my son and I took a look at the cat?"

"Oh, not at all. That what you wanted? Come on in, fella. We've got her frozen out back."

He led them through the brightly lit room of desks and wall maps without introducing them to two other officers in their khaki uniforms who sat smoking and drinking coffee and staring.

On the back porch of the building there was a big freezer humming away. Crane reached up for the light string and a bare bulb flashed on. Then he opened the lid.

To fit her inside, they had formed her body in the shape of a dog begging, with her paws bent back beneath her chin, her hind legs curled up, and her long tail twisted along her stomach. Her eyes were shut.

"She's a beauty," Crane said.

Moses stared down in silence. After a while he reached into the freezer and touched her ear.

"Mr. Crane?" he said, straightening up.

"Yes sir?"

"As you may know, my people . . . are a very religious people."

"Yes?"

"Well, it's hard to explain, but the panther is important to their religion."

"I see. That's the old religion you're talking about now, isn't it?"

"Yes. Yes, that's right. What I'm coming to is this. We need a panther such as this one. I know that sounds strange to you, and all. I can't explain what it means completely . . . because it's secret. But we need it. We sure do."

"You mean you need—you want—*this* cat?"

"Yes. We do."

Crane cleared his throat.

"I don't have jurisdiction of the body, Mr. Raincrow."

"You don't have...? Who does, then?"

"Well, my parent agency."

"Who do I talk to, then?"

"Talk to? Lemme see, Raincrow." He slowly closed the freezer lid, pulled the light off, and walked inside. They followed him on into the room where the other men sat.

"Pete," Crane said to one of them, "these Indians want the cat for their religion. What do you say to that?"

Pete was a smallish, pudgy man with thinning hair and red cheeks. He cut his narrow, dark eyes at the other two white men and smiled. Then he eased his swivel desk chair around to face Moses.

"What kind of religion do you call that?" he asked in a high, precise voice.

"It's ours," Moses said.

"I told them," Crane said, "that the body belongs to the agency, in a manner of speaking."

"In a manner of speaking?" Moses asked.

"Do you want to *worship* the body?" Pete asked in his tenor.

"No," Moses replied. "We do not."

"Because if you do, that's idolatry."

Moses waited.

"It's hard to say who owns the body, Mr. Raincrow," Crane finally said to him. "I mean, there's always another level up."

"I wouldn't ever want to be part of such a thing," Pete said.

"We are asking on behalf of the Miccosukee people," Moses said wearily.

The third white man was big and had a pitted face. "Reckon what they want with that body?" he asked to nobody in particular.

"Eldon," Pete said, "I hate to think."

"Who is in authority over the cat's remains?" Moses asked, the temper finally coming into his voice.

"To tell you the truth, Mr. Raincrow," Crane said, "I don't know. You could write a letter to the director of the Endangered Species Task Force and make your request that way. But I can tell you right now what's going to be done with this panther."

"And what is that?"

"She's headed up to the university lab on the next refrigeration truck that comes this way. Research. Got to study every specimen we get, Mr. Raincrow. Got to learn all we can about the cats if we're going to have a chance to save them."

"You mean there's nobody in charge? You can't name me one individual I can talk to?"

"I can name you some," Crane said stiffly. "But I can guarantee you what the disposition of this animal will be."

"Guarantee me?" Moses said, his voice rising a notch.

"Absolutely."

Moses turned and surveyed Eldon and Pete; they

were watching him with a mixture of amusement and challenge.

"If we released this body to the unknown practices of heathenism," Pete said, "no telling what would be said about us."

"Heathenism," Eldon repeated to himself.

"Unknown savage heathenism," Pete said.

Moses started for the door.

"Look," Crane said, catching Moses' arm and stopping him. But he seemed embarrassed to speak before the others. "Let me walk you out," he mumbled.

Then, beside the truck, he spoke softly to them. "I'm sorry about those boys," he said. "They're just local boys who work for me. I mean, they aren't trained to handle anything special. And I'm sorry this panther got killed today, and I'm sorry you drove up here for nothing. But I work for the government—you can see that—and I can't take it upon myself to give away official property."

"Sure," Moses said.

They climbed into the cab and slammed their doors, and Moses turned the key. Crane stood outlined against the porch light, his long arms close to his angled body, his hands in his pockets, watching them turn and pull onto the blacktop. John looked back and saw Eldon and Pete join him on the porch, clear in the yellow light, shaking their heads at each other. And then they burst out laughing.

Purification

Moses got his truck up to seventy miles an hour before he lifted his heavy boot from the accelerator.

They rode for ten miles before he was able to speak.

"How'd you like that, son?" he asked in a rasp. "How'd you like being called a heathen and a savage?"

A few miles later he said, "When they decided to put the panther on their Endangered Species list, did they come before the tribal council and ask us to support that? *No!* They mailed us a flier *telling* us about it. We probably would have supported it, too. Because it seemed like a good idea. But they just rammed it down our throats."

Moses swerved to miss a rabbit that ran across in the headlights.

"But I've been abiding by it, haven't I?"

"Yes."

"That's right. As much as I need a panther, I've been trying to cooperate with their law."

"I know you have," John said, "because there're only thirty left."

"Even if there's only *ten*, son, and my religion calls for me to take one ... they come out here and build their highways and run the panther down at night. A highway patrolman even hit one—how about the irony of that?"

"I know."

"And how many have Crane and his bunch killed with their dogs and their radio collars?"

"I'll bet *he's* the only one who knows that," John said.

"You're right, son. I'll bet you're dead right about that."

Moses raised his right fist and shook it. "Ahhhhhhhhhhhh!" he yelled.

They didn't speak again until they saw the dark front of Sedie's little store in the distance, and Moses began to slow down. He came to a stop and cut the lights and motor. They sat together for a moment, and Moses rested his forehead on the steering wheel.

"All right," he said steadily when he straightened up. "Here's what I'm going to do. I'm going to take a sweat tonight. I'm going to ask the Breathmaker for guidance. Then I'm going out with my rifle in the morning. If the panther wants to come to me ... if he wants to do it ... be my Give Away ... then I'll take him."

"That's good."

"It's not like I'm going to force it. I'm not going

to run him with dogs. And I'm not going to wait up in trees like Max. I don't have time, for one thing. But I'll go out tomorrow morning, and we'll just see what happens."

"I'll help you," John said.

"How? With the sweat?"

"Yes. And you know I had that dream about the panther last night . . . and then I saw him this morning. . . . I'm not sure, but the pasture *looked* just like the one in my dream."

"Maybe the Sky Panthers are working through you in some way."

"Maybe so." John was uncomfortable at this thought. "Anyway," he said, "if they want to send me another dream tonight, I'll be ready for it."

Moses took John's shoulder in his hand and held it for a long time.

▲▲▲ When they reached the camp, John and Moses walked down the trail in the blackness to the sweat lodge. Together they built the fire, and Moses heated the pumice stones while John gathered water.

They stripped and Moses threw the first bucketful over the stones, and the hut filled with steam.

In a moment they could barely see each other through the fog.

"Papa, I was thinking about something," John said. "You know the little buck I brought in for Grandmother."

"Yes."

"Well, I was wondering if his skin would be all right for the medicine bundle."

Moses leaned on his fist, elbow on knee, and looked at John through the gloom. "Instead of the old buck?"

"Yes."

"Why? You don't want to kill him?"

"Well, I just wondered if we have to."

"We have to," Moses said. "It's good that you don't take pleasure from it, though."

"But you were going to use the panther *they* killed."

Moses sat up straight very slowly as he spoke.

"You mean, since I didn't shoot her myself..."

"Yes."

He sighed. "I know, son. Most likely her medicine wouldn't have worked for me. But I was hoping. I was going to try it. A medicine keeper is supposed to kill his own panther. Because that way, the Sky Spirits appear to him. They give a sign."

"In the Give Away."

"Yes."

"Why do you want *me* to kill the old buck?"

"Well...I was hoping...you know, I was hoping for a long time...you might take an interest in my medicine work. I had the idea that the buck would never show himself to you unless it was supposed to be."

"But if he did?"

"Then maybe you'd feel the power in you. And the calling."

"Oh."

Moses nodded. He got up and brought them another bucket of water. Then the rocks exploded in steam, and they sat together without talking, using their energy to breathe.

∧∧∧∧∧∧∧∧∧∧∧∧∧∧∧∧∧∧∧ 14
Faith and Doubt

Moses brought John out of sleep very slowly. Just touching his shoulder, whispering in a distant voice, he asked, "John? Do you see the panther? Look around him. What do you see, son? Where is he?"

And John, hearing the voice and not knowing where it was coming from, saw the panther for an instant, standing against the broad stump of a great bald cypress tree.

Then he was sitting up, and his mouth was dry, and he realized he was in the chickee.

"Did you see anything?"

"Yes. He was in cypress woods. With huge stumps. The biggest stumps you ever saw."

They were both trying to think.

"The biggest?" Moses suddenly said.

They grinned together in the darkness.

"Could it be where Grandfather Charlie got the log for his last canoe?" Moses asked.

"It must be! The stumps were that big!"

"Shhhhh!" Moses said, glancing at Mary in her sleep. "All right. That's what we were hoping for."

"Did you have a dream?" John asked.

"Nothing," his father said as he moved away to the fire.

They sat for a moment, rubbing their hands against the chill in the air. *"I'm* supposed to take the panther, and he appears in *your* dream—twice now."

John shrugged. Moses took a dipper of *sofkee,* the thin gruel allowed even during fasts, and gave it to his son.

"We'll go there," Moses whispered, "and if he comes, he comes. Then we'll know that we were supposed to do it together. Because I never would have thought of that place."

▲▲▲ Then they were in the moving, silent canoe, Moses poling up the still water, John in the bow hugging his arms against the dampness. Moses' fine, single-shot .270 lay in its soft case between them.

Very far away, on the fringe of hearing, an alligator roared, and crows cawed angrily in the darkness.

And a half hour later, in first light, they beached the dugout on a spit of sand. Moses led the way through a pine thicket, with the crowns of the trees joining above them. The underbrush had been cleared out by years of shade, and it was like walking in a fresh-smelling park.

Finally they came to a marsh of sawgrass and

turned to follow a trail around its dry edge toward the trees on the far side.

When they were near the woods, Moses stopped and tested the breeze. They sat down together in the sage grass, facing each other, as the gray light diffused and clarified into real morning. Moses took out his long ceremonial pipe and filled it.

He looked up at the blue sky.

"Grandfathers," he said, "we have come here to ask for one of your panthers for our medicine. We ask you to deliver this cat to us, for the healing of our sick, for frightening off the deer and rabbits that cause sickness.

"We ask for this animal for the good of our tribe, Grandfathers."

Moses lit the pipe, took a single puff, and passed it to John. John held it, drew one breath through it, and returned it to his father.

"If it is the will of the Breathmaker," Moses said, "and of the Sky Panthers, then send us the Give Away this morning. We are sorry to take the life of our brother, but it is the old way, and it will fulfill our friendship with the Panther Grandfathers. It will be a sign to all the people that the old hunting magic is alive. And it will help drive the deer from Grandmother Mary."

Then Moses wrapped up his pipe and put it away.

From the pocket of his jeans he slipped out a single rifle cartridge and held it in his fingers between them.

"This is the only one I brought," he said. "If they

want us to have a Give Away, it's the only one we'll need."

John nodded gravely.

"I'll meet you here midmorning," his father said.

∧∧∧ Moses took the rifle and walked into the trees. They were tall, thin, second-growth cypresses with wispy crowns, and they had risen after the destruction of the ancient monsters whose stumps still sat like great flat stones on the surface of the earth. These trees had been the last of the original timber on the reservation, and when they were cut forty years ago, one of them had fallen into a deep slough and was left. When Moses' grandfather had decided to make a last dugout canoe before he died, he had remembered that log. It was seasoned then, hardened, and he got a crew of men to haul it out with oxen. Then he did his slow, beautiful work with the adz and the hatchet, carving the final one he would make.

So these woods had always been special to Moses, and he was pleased that John's dream had foreseen the panther here. Moses slipped over the soft cypress needles of the woods floor, listening, and he wondered where he should take his stand.

There was a fallen tree with its roots upended in soft mud, a casualty of windstorms and rain-soaked ground. It made a good, dry place to sit, and here he could face the open woods of wide, dark stumps and thin, young trees.

Moses pulled out his knife and cut stalks of

switchcane and stuck them up in a circle around his spot, to make a blind. Then he took his seat, the rifle across his lap, his thumb resting on the safety. He began to wait.

At first he was expectant, knowing that sometimes the Give Away will come almost the minute you sit down. As he listened and watched, the trees seemed to hide panthers everywhere. Sharp, pointed shadows looked like ears, and hopping squirrels sounded like the padding of quick, heavy feet. But the first hour passed and the woods were still empty. And Moses began to doubt and was thrown back upon himself.

Do I deserve this panther? The question could not be avoided, but Moses was sure that it would be unwise to answer it. He could not pronounce himself purified, prepared, deserving. Even to think about these things was dangerous. His job was to observe the ceremonies before the hunt and to wait in peace and patience, concentrating on the form of his hunting, not the animal he hoped to bring home.

If I can kill this panther, using only hunting magic, the news will spread like a fire among the people. They'll be amazed. I'll be amazed. And my personal medicine power will be confirmed.

Would the word get outside the tribe? Moses faced the fact that this was unavoidable. Still, what was the worst that could happen? The reservation was off limits to government game officials. The fine and jail terms couldn't apply to him, a Native

American on tribal land. So he didn't have to worry about the consequences outside the tribe. He wouldn't want this to start a pattern, though. He wouldn't want young hotshots like Max Poor Bear to start panther hunting. Maybe he would have to go before the council and suggest a ruling of their own.

Was there anything else to worry about? Well, his excitement, his pride. *How much of this is my religious duty?* he wondered. *And how much is about the men of our tribe?* He smiled. *So I'm not as pure in my heart as I'd like to believe,* he admitted to himself. *And I'm glad this duty has fallen upon me.*

A yellowhammer landed on the log near Moses and drilled into its hard surface for bugs.

Still, he thought, *if that's what it's about, I don't deserve one. And the Sky Panthers won't send one.*

A loud horsefly buzzed Moses' face, circled around his head three times, and landed on his hair.

My part is not to ask questions, he said to himself, unmoving, enduring the fly, keeping watch for a change anywhere in the field of his vision. *My part is only to wait, to hunt,* he said to himself. *What the Sky Panthers want to make of this moment is up to them.*

AAAAAAAAAAAAAAAAAAA 15

Over the Bones of the Past

The panther was far from the cypress brake. He had returned during the night to the place where his mate had been killed and he had recoiled from the urine of dogs, the oily tracks of leather boots, the smell of death. He shook himself and ran through the swamp for a long time, splashing across a leafy pond, rolling over and over in dry, aromatic cypress needles in a dense thicket, scratching the sweet sticky sap from beneath the bark of a hard, yellow pine. Finally he smelled only of the woods and the night air.

Then he had traveled south. Once he thought he heard his mate in a canebrake, and he whistled in reply, but it was only a mockingbird, and without her scent to hold him there, he loped on.

When he came to the edge of the highway at dawn, he stopped and listened. There was no sound but the morning birds in first light, and he jumped the wide watery ditch and scrambled up the bank to the black trail. There was a sudden whine to his right.

Frozen in place, he saw two fiery eyes focused on him. They were far away at first, but in an instant they had grown into bright suns and the whine was increasing with a roar underneath it. He crouched and his ears went flat. He jerked forward and then backward for an inch, but he held his spot, his brain racing with the confusion of this beast, and then the eighteen-wheeler was towering toward him, its eyes shooting out long shafts of clear, white light. It was going to pass just beyond but it swerved into his side of the trail, jumping with amazing quickness for such a giant, and he was frozen as the light shafts caught and held him.

Then he sprang backward in the air with all his strength, wrenching his back and falling in the hot wind of the long-sided beast. He fell into the darkness behind its eyes, not just down on the hard trail but over the embankment, too, crashing into cool water and mud and briers.

He clawed and spit and ran out of the wet hole, leaping into gray scrub and taking a needle stab of yucca in his right shoulder. He flinched and dodged away from it, arcing high into the air over another spiky plant, and raced on. Finally he stood shivering in the shadow of a great live oak tree, its low heavy limbs dripping with beards of Spanish moss and orchids.

He trotted north, back the way he had come that morning.

The panther was in the center of his territory,

and his impulse was to mark its boundaries again. He would urinate at regular intervals around its perimeter, daring any male cat to enter and try to cross.

He still trembled from the wound in his shoulder, but he was growing calmer now, and he struck an old trail around a marsh where he usually met rabbits. Within half a mile a rabbit ran straight into him, and he batted at it in surprise with his paw. The rabbit darted between his legs and disappeared as a blur into the cane and blackberry briers beside the trail. Now the panther tore after him, but a rope of brier caught the dead radio collar around his neck, jerking his windpipe and making him fight to rip himself free. The rabbit was a long way gone when the cat emerged from the thicket, standing in the open, licking the tender spot on the point of his shoulder.

And then something happened.

The big panther began to move along the trail, following the marsh edge as if something were waiting for him ahead. It was not the smell of a deer or a rabbit, nothing like the scent of a female of his own kind, but it drew him steadily in the brightening morning, and when he passed the hot scent of a whole cluster of rabbits sleeping nearby, he didn't even turn his head.

When he had rounded the wide marsh he turned due north again. Perhaps a new cat had invaded his ground. Whatever it was, it compelled him, and he ran out into an open pasture of green grass, crossing it without caution in the early sun. When he entered the Green Thicket, where his mate had died, he hardly noticed the cold smells there. His morning lay ahead.

He ran on into pine woods, sparse and clean, and as he crossed in the shadows he came to a small grassy field within the trees. It was sandy there, with clumps of reddish sagegrass growing, and the panther stopped, trembling, in its center. Far down below him in the ground there was a great bone pile, thirty thousand years old, of the skeletons of tigers. They were the long-vanished saber-toothed cats, clustered here in a mysterious mass grave beneath the layers of the earth. There were many of these tiger graves hidden in the Everglades, and on this clear morning, as the big panther stopped and squinted, a tremor passed through him. He belonged to this place. It was bred into him, and into all his blood-kin felines, after millions of years of living through the flesh of deer and rabbits in this swamp. The patches of light and shadow in his blinking vision were his own camouflage, his own skin as he moved. The breath of wind over the sagegrass was his own grace. The presence of ancient tigers filled him, called him to great slabs of cut cypress trunks, rising like stones above the black mud of the woods floor. He knew that place well, but what was there? That was the source of his feeling and his calling. He growled once and ran to meet it.

AAAAAAAAAAAAAAAAAAAA **16**

Ceremony of the Panther

Moses knew his time was running out. He had waited in perfect stillness since dawn, and now he judged there was a ten-o'clock sun. His back hurt, and he needed to stretch. Soon he would have to meet John.

But he had served his time on the fallen log, he had watched every second, and he could be proud of that. He knew he had hunted well. So if it was not meant to be, then that was it. Perhaps the Sky Panthers hadn't liked the way he'd approached it, without scouting even a little.

Maybe they're teaching me a lesson, he thought, *letting me sit out here and watch the bluejays.*

He would give it ten more minutes.

It was strange to him how the ending of a hunt was so different from the beginning: At first you expected success, and it was easy to keep alert, to keep watch. The swamp was like an open door, through which the animals would step at any moment. You felt invisible and strong. But now, in the closing of it, the woods felt endless and empty, the animals seemed to be sleeping in distant thickets, and no spirits seemed to care. It was only the careful way he had hunted that kept him from despair.

Then there was motion.

It was a thing...low, long, running in the trees ...brown like a deer...crossing the cypresses almost a hundred yards away. Moses got the rifle to his shoulder in one quick, smooth instant, safety catch off, and he picked an alley in the trees just ahead of the moving form. He exhaled his drawn breath, laid the black crosshairs of the old scope on that single distant spot, and when it was momentarily filled he squeezed the trigger.

The loud solid crack of the rifle echoed for a long time against the hard trunks of the trees.

ΛΛΛ John came running. He reached the spot where they had left each other, and took a line straight into the woods. Since there had been only one cartridge, the hunt with the rifle was over. It had already happened. Either his father had done it, or he had missed, or—horrible to even think— he had wounded a panther.

Now John was into the dark trees, and he stopped to listen. No sound. The birds were hushed.

He whistled tentatively, a high note and then a lower, falling one, their old signal.

Moses answered.

John ran again, bearing toward the sound, praying with every step.

And in the distance he saw his father in a patch of sunlight, holding the rifle to his chest, standing over the body of the cat.

It was unbelievable.

He reached his father and they couldn't stop grinning, and they couldn't take their eyes off the long, beautiful panther. Only one thing marred it, the ugly radio collar, and Moses dropped to his knees and removed it, then flung it away into the shadows.

John sat beside the magnificent square head of the cat and smoothed his fur back. His face was marked with black lines around his nose and lips, his chin was white, and his whiskers were long and fine. The .270 had made a single clean hole just behind his shoulder.

When John looked at his father again, the smile was gone.

"Son," Moses said, "Let's remember why we're here."

John nodded.

"We need to give thanks, right now."

They sat down cross-legged in the leaves, with the cat between them.

Moses opened his arms to the sky. "Grandfathers," he said, "we give thanks for this moment. We are grateful to the spirit of this panther, who has made a Give Away of his life for our people.

"We thank the Sky Panthers for sending him to us, a sacrifice, that Grandmother Mary and others might be delivered of the deer sickness, and have life.

"And we thank the Breathmaker, Giver of All Things, for our lives, and for this opportunity to serve our people with the panther's medicine."

Moses slowly lowered his arms. He took out his long pipe, filled and lit it, and he and John took a single puff each.

Then they sat together beside the panther for a long time. Neither of them wanted to break the spell. John knew that such a moment might never come to them again.

▲▲▲▲▲▲▲▲▲▲▲▲▲▲▲▲▲▲▲▲▲ 17

The Give Away

The sound of Officer Crane's air boat had faded from hearing, and John was still holding his great-grandmother when his mother came walking back into camp. She moved slowly, like an old woman, and her head was down.

"They wouldn't take you with them," John asked.

"No."

"I've got the dugout. I'll take you."

"What good will you do him?" Grandmother Mary asked sadly.

"I don't know!" John snapped. "How can I know that?"

"I can tell you what will help Moses more than anything," Grandmother Mary said. "And it's something you need to do out here."

"Oh?" he said.

"You know, don't you?"

"Yes."

His mother came up beside them and laid her

hand on his arm. "I can pole myself to Sedie's," she said. "I don't mind. I'll call the tribal lawyers from there and figure out what to do next."

"It just seems like I ought to be with you," John said.

Grandmother Mary released him and stood up angrily. She was shaky, and he held her hand. "You have no place in that world!" she said. "Out here there's something to be done!" She pushed away from him and walked unsteadily toward the trail to the canal.

John faced his mother.

"She wants me to kill the old buck in the Green Thicket," he said. "She and Papa say I should do it. They want his skin for the medicine pack."

Anna nodded. He watched her sad, pretty face and her tired eyes.

"They say I have to do it, just like Papa had to kill the panther."

His mother waited for him to go on.

"What do you think?" he asked.

"Me?" She smiled slightly and walked away from him. Then she made a big, slow circle, holding her hands together. "You know what?" she said as she returned to him; "that's the first time in a *long* time anybody's asked what I thought about these things."

John was surprised.

"Your father's medicine work...I support him, you know that."

"Yes."

"But this whole idea of your going his way...I know he wants it so much, and so does Mary."

John sighed and nodded.

"But you can't do it for them, can you?"

"No."

"If you feel it, and that's what you want, then go on, son. They say the Sky Spirits choose the man ...not the other way around."

He studied her face, as if her true beliefs might somehow show there.

"Don't ask me what to do!" She laughed for an instant.

"You're nearly grown now, anyway." She waited while he took this in. "And don't put me in the *middle!*" she said.

He laughed with her, and then her worry lines returned. "I've got to get started," she said. "I don't think you have to stay out here to look after Mary ...she's been fine for the last forty years on this island! But if you want to stay and work things out with the deer...that's up to you."

John walked beside her down to the canal. Grandmother Mary was sitting on the edge of the dugout.

"What's he doing here?" she said, eyes in a squint at John.

"Ask him," Anna said. She climbed into the bow and slipped back into her seat, her hands around the long cypress pole.

Grandmother Mary stood up. "Well?" she growled.

"I'm just telling Mama good-bye," he said. He leaned down and slid the canoe backward off the mud and sand, out into the channel.

▲▲▲ Before dawn the next morning he was lying on his back in the darkness, eyes open. He was alert, smelling the clean water of the glades, listening for something.

The breeze came over him all of a sudden, startling and cool, and he sat up straight. He was not surprised he'd awakened on time.

But he had no dream in his mind. Slowly, he lay back down and closed his eyes. He breathed deeply, relaxed his whole body, and watched the field of darkness. It was easy to see the old buck—but only in his imagination. The images didn't have that feel of strange reality, of revelation.

So he got up and took a dipper of *sofkee*, and then opened his great-grandfather's ancient trunk. The rifle was in there, wrapped in a yellowed alligator skin; it was a .35 Remington, an old model they hadn't made for fifty years. He felt inside the pouch for the fat, tarnished cartridges he had once watched Moses fire at targets. Though the rifle would hold five, he took only one.

Soon he was wading waist-deep along the edge of the canal toward the Green Thicket. He would return to where he had seen the panther, or maybe hunt in the woods beyond, where Max had killed those deer. Since the Sky Spirits hadn't sent him a dream, he would go to the place of his old Hunt

Dream, and if they wanted to present him with the buck...

It was a damp morning, with a shifty breeze. First light began to filter into the air, and he heard thrushes cawing in the button bushes and, high in a palm tree, a mockingbird's song.

He waded steadily, and by the time he reached his destination there was good walking light. Then he slipped up into the cutover pines and soon was facing the green pasture.

It was so huge and still and empty! He stood there for a few minutes, scanning the distant edges of the woods, almost surprised that no deer were in sight. Then he decided to cross it. He would hunt in the trees on the far side, in the Green Thicket itself.

By the time he had walked in long strides across the field and found an open place in the trees with a fallen log to sit on, he was warmed up. And he had a clear view, facing almost directly into the tricky breeze. His tiredness was spread evenly through his body now, and it was almost a pleasant feeling, like a drowsy trance, as he settled in.

The important thing, Moses always said, was how you hunted. Whether you killed anything didn't matter—that was up to the Sky Spirits, anyway. *Sky Spirits,* John thought. *Are there really any such things?*

He watched a big, gray squirrel on the side of a pine tree. It ran rapidly up the slick, scaly bark to a high limb, stood on its hind legs, and grabbed a cone that was growing from a little branch. It took its time, cutting the pine cone apart in slow, deliberate nibbles, letting the individual seeds fall, spinning, to the forest floor below.

John sighed and fixed his gaze on the open woods before him. *It's an open door, Papa always said. Through it, all the animals of the glades might come. Will come—if they're supposed to, and if you're worthy.*

John realized he was looking straight at a deer.

It was a small buck, only forty or so yards away from him, standing right out in the open and watching back over its shoulder. It was beautiful, its gray-and-white colors seeming washed and even brushed in perfect lines. Where had it come from? And why hadn't it made even one sound?

The deer lowered his head and took an acorn in his teeth, raised up again quickly, and crunched the acorn as he studied the woods behind him. There must be another deer back there.

This was not the Give Away, John knew. And he was grateful it was not. That decision was always left up to the hunter, to know when a deer was an offering and when it was there before you simply by accident. In that case, to kill it would be wrong.

So it was a great pleasure just to watch the little buck, who was not as careful as he should have been.

Max would never let him go like this. John smiled. The buck snorted and jumped, flicked his tail, stared behind him, and then relaxed again. John saw that the sides of his body had a light, reddish-brown sheen over the gray undercoat of fur. He took another acorn and cracked it, and his ears moved this way and that, trying to pick up the slightest sounds.

The buck stamped his foot once, snorted lightly, and tipped on off through the trees, as if he had an appointment and had just realized he was late. John felt grateful he had seen the deer up so close, and he wished another one would appear. He wished he could quit thinking of Max.

The breeze came again, and the squirrel ran across the leafy ground carrying an acorn in its mouth. A big, red-and-black pileated woodpecker landed on a pine stump, drilled into its soft wood for a few moments, and then flew on. John was glad he was out here today, far from highways and alligator shows, far from whites, just hidden in the swamp. He knew he'd never go back to the Trail and to Max Poor Bear.

The trees moved gently in the wind, and they seemed alive, each with its own patient spirit. *The tree spirits watch over you, son, Grandmother Mary always said. They send messages, from one to the other, and let me know about you, wherever you are.*

Today it felt true. It felt possible.

Then the great buck came. He was loping gracefully through the distant trunks, where shafts of morning sunlight had begun to penetrate the dense shadows. His horns, when he crossed in a patch of light, were bright and yellow and clear in a high circle above his head. He turned and ran straight toward John, then veered a little to the left, but he kept coming faster and faster.

He grew larger as he came on, filling the spaces between the trees, and he was as close as the little buck had been when he suddenly ran behind a thick clump of cypress and didn't come out. He had stopped there, with one hard thump against the soft earth, and then there was silence. John's heart was flying. He took the safety catch off the rifle and raised it to his shoulder, sighting into the space beyond the trees. This was his one chance, before the buck's eye reappeared, seeing everything. John took his deep breath.

Moses will be so proud of you, Grandmother Mary had said without saying.

The buck stepped out cautiously, his neck thick and curved, alertness and dignity radiating from him as if he owned the woods, as if he could feel the heartbeat of anything there. His black, knowing eye stopped on John.

Do this for him, Grandmother had meant.

The buck was going to be there only for another second. John lined up the iron sights on his shoulder and breathed out, then touched the cold, smooth trigger.

He's a gift, John could hear Moses saying. He's a gift of the Sky Deer for the medicine bundle.

Every muscle of the buck quivered as he felt his enemy's presence. He cocked his head, his vision fixed on John's form, and he stamped his hoof one time and crouched to spring away. But something held him there, held him trembling and frozen and exposed to the sighted rifle of the Miccosukee hunter, who was without motion or sound or even breath on the fallen log.

In that instant John felt the power of the Sky Spirits filling him. The rifle of his dead great-grandfather became their instrument. And the single cartridge in its chamber connected his soul to the soul of the buck. The breeze moved over them like the hand of the Breathmaker, joining them into one being, and their eyes together knew everything.

"*Go!*" John said as he lowered the rifle. And the buck made a quick dodge and then stopped again, this time with eyes wild and astonished, with indecision flashing through him. John raised his hand in a grave way, palm out to the buck, and in a strong voice, he said, "*Go, Grandfather, go now.*"

And this time the buck leaped and flew in a crooked pattern through the woods and through the air, and in a moment there was just the flickering of his white tail, far off in the silent trees.

John stood up and cradled the rifle in his arms.

A gust of wind swept through the tops high above him, swishing their branches together and admitting splashes of morning light. As much as it was a hunter's duty to be purified before the hunt, and as much as it was the duty of Sky Deer to make a gift of one of their own, there was still another duty to be observed. It was a hunter's decision, and only his decision, about the Give Away. It was only he who knew, who could ever know, whether to accept.

And in that moment something else was finally clear. He was released from the burden of his father's path, the medicine path. He would assist Moses at the Green Corn Dance and in his healing ceremonies as well, but that was all. John would never claim the spirit call he didn't feel.

The Sky Deer showed me the old buck for another reason, for some other reason, he thought as he stepped over the dry, fallen branches and pushed the vines aside. *They want me to use the young buck's skin for the medicine bundle,* he heard himself telling his father. *I'm going to prepare it for you.*

He headed out of the woods the way he had come, trying to imagine Moses' response.

John was smiling as he crossed the wide green field.